IMPERFECT MOMENTS

Candis Graham

IMPERFECT MOMENTS

Candis Graham

June 1993

Germaine

POLESTAR
BOOK PUBLISHERS

Imperfect Moments

© 1993 Candis Graham

Published by
Polestar Book Publishers
2758 Charles Street
Vancouver, BC   V5K 3A7

Distributed in Canada by
Raincoast Books
112 East Third Avenue
Vancouver, BC   V5T 1C8

Earlier versions of the following stories have been previously published: "Delila and Ms. MacLeod" appeared as "Nothing Special" in **Women and Words: The Anthology/Les Femmes et les Mots: Une Anthologie,** Harbour Publishing Co. Ltd., 1984; "Aprons and Homemade Bread" in **Dykeversions,** The Women's Press, 1986; "Elle-même With Waves" in **By word of mouth,** gynergy books, 1989 and *Rites,* July/August 1989; "A Guilty Move" in *Common Lives/Lesbian Lives,* No. 33, Winter 1990 and *GO INFO,* No. 145, March 1992; "Scots Pine and Cranberry Chains" appeared as "Because" in **Tide Lines,** gynergy books, 1991; "Imperfect Moments" in *Grain,* 1993.

Cover art and design by Watermoon Design Inc.
Author photograph by W. Clouthier
Editing and production by Michelle Benjamin
Printed in Canada

Canadian Cataloguing in Publication Data
Graham, Candis J. (Candis Jean), 1949-
Imperfect moments

ISBN 0-919591-47-7

1. Women—Fiction. 2. Lesbians—Fiction.
I. Title.
PS8563.R33I4 1993   C813'.54   C93-091003-6
PR9199.3.G72I4 1993

As well as thanking my lucky stars, I wish to thank a few divine women . . .

Barb Augustine — for sending my work to a real writer in 1980 and other forms of sustenance through the years.

Brenda Brooks — for the 1991 readings and the 1992 music and the ongoing revelry.

J.A. Hamilton and Marian Frances White — for their letters from both coasts and the occasional flying visit.

Kim Nash — for the lunch-time conversations about the business of being a bookseller and, more recently, for telling me to talk to Michelle.

Lynne Westlake — for the neverending stimulating conversations on a zillion topics and for showing me gentle kindness.

Margaret Graham and Mary Meigs — for providing me with the money to attend *West Word Two* in Victoria, 1986, and Sandy Frances Duncan for being there.

Margaret Telegdi — for introducing me to conscious feminism in 1974 and setting a fine example ever since.

Michelle Benjamin — for having the courage to take this on, sight unseen, and for her gracious presence and timely advice throughout.

Patricia Ginn — for giving me a place to live and write during the summer of 1979.

And . . . *Fireweed* and *The Canadian Forum* for recommending me for Ontario Arts Council grants in 1991, and Women's Press for the 1992 recommendation.

for Wendy Irene Mary Mary

IMPERFECT MOMENTS

Imperfect Moments

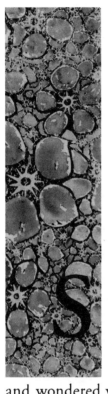

She had dirt under her nails. I knew the dark lines were dirt because she had planted her garden the day before.

I looked down at my own clean nails and wondered why it is earth when we plant seeds in a garden but becomes dirt when it is under our nails. I decided I would not say anything. I did not want to call attention to her dirty fingernails.

I watched her large hands shake the glass bottle and pour the dressing. It was a delicious-smelling vinaigrette made with olive oil and raspberry vinegar. Eating at Fiona's place is a pleasure in every sense. She is a gifted cook, a natural, and each meal is different from the other as if she has an endless store of ideas and recipes. And she knows how to arrange food so it looks delectable.

I propped my elbows on the table and rested my face in my hands. "What's that smell?"

"It's the lilies of the valley." She nodded in the direction of a squat round white bowl at the other end of her kitchen table. It was overflowing with white lilies of the valley and blue forget-me-nots. "Don't they make a wonderful stink. I liked that vase at first sight, although it has a slight crack that leaks minute amounts of water. I noticed the crack when I bought it, but I couldn't resist. Do you ever feel like that, you see something and want it no matter what?" She put the cork back in the bottle and used two large wooden spoons to toss the lettuce, spinach, parsley, grated cheese, rings of red onion, tomato wedges and walnuts. "It's an impulse with no reason or sense."

I reached into the salad bowl and took a piece of walnut. "I suppose I feel that way about music. I hear something and like it and want to buy it immediately so I can listen to it over and over whenever I want." I popped the walnut into my mouth.

"Yes, I suppose it comes down to a feeling and good music arouses feelings." Fiona gathered up spoonfuls of salad and filled my plate. "I think the vase suits those flowers perfectly but I didn't know that when I bought it. I only use it twice a year, around this time for the lilies of the valley and forget-me-nots and then again at Christmas to hold a little pot of poinsettia. It warms my heart to see the scarlet flowers coming out of that pure whiteness." She smiled. "That's why it sits on that wad of folded tea towel, to absorb the slow leak."

I looked at the salad on my plate and realized my mouth was filled with saliva. "I like lilies of the valley."

"Aren't they exquisite. And they have such a wonderful scent. But a garden is so much work. When I was cutting those flowers this morning I found weeds coming up. I

have to admire weeds because they grow almost everywhere, but," she gave a little laugh, "getting rid of them is
exhausting work."

I picked up my fork. "Are you ever tempted to just let
them grow?"

"No. Never. I'll go out this weekend and pull them out
by the roots, every last one of them."

I knew too, from the moment I noticed dark lines
under her fingernails, that she is a woman who does not
set great store by appearances. She puts thought into her
wardrobe and dresses with care, and she has a good sense
of colour. But I know that she barely glances at herself in
the mirror while brushing her hair and massaging cream
into the dry skin of her hands. She does not dip her
fingertips into tiny pots of colour or fiddle patiently with
tubes and sponges and cakes and brushes. I knew this
without ever having been around when she starts her day.

Sitting beside her at that kitchen table I realized I have
known this about her since we first met three years ago. I
knew this, but had never thought about it until I noticed
the dark crescents beneath her nails. I felt a rush of
warmth for her. My impulse was to reach out and touch
her, to express my love without words or pretence.

The moment passed. I reached into the salad bowl to
take another piece of walnut and our conversation turned
to plans for the summer. She said she was going to a cottage on a small lake north of Peterborough for the month
of July, to sit with her feet in the lake and her nose in a
book for a whole month.

I poured myself a cup of steaming tea from her plump
white tea pot, which is decorated with splashes of water-
colour-like purple flowers. I told her I was planning to

spend my holidays sitting in my hot and extremely humid living room, working on my novel. I reached for another bun from the pottery bowl of broad pink and red stripes. I pulled the bun open and smoothed margarine in the soft insides.

I didn't ask if David was going to the cottage. I assumed he would be there.

Sometimes we talk about me being lesbian. She seems curious and usually initiates these conversations. I don't know if her interest is personal or if it comes from her general inquisitiveness about people. I sense that she loves women as only a lesbian can.

I try to be open when we talk, but at the back of my mind I know she shares her life with a man and I am hesitant to reveal much. I can never be entirely open with her because of him.

Yet I treasure her loving friendship. She is much more than a friend. Or perhaps I mean that what we have is rare because she is truly a friend? I feel I could ask anything of her. I have never done this, but I know I could. I could phone her and she would respond immediately. If she called on me I would do the same for her. If only she would declare her love for women . . . but that is wishful thinking.

Later, after we had eaten the marvellous salad with the vinaigrette dressing and home-made macaroni with cheese (which she made because she knows I love macaroni and cheese so much that I'll even eat the kind that comes out of a box with a foil package of powdered fluorescent cheese) and the wholewheat buns, after I had left her and gone home, I remembered her hands. They are long and generous. I imagined her gathering earth carefully around a green stem and patting the ground as she murmurs encouraging words to a young plant.

Although she is primarily a practical woman, she does not plant a practical garden. She does not plant food. No potatoes, lettuce, cucumbers, carrots, peas, green onions or tomatoes. She plants flowers.

Beside her back door are two bushy peony plants, one on either side of the step. Fat buds burst into full shocking-pink blossoms every June. Along her back fence is a wide bed of assorted perennials and a few annuals. She has planned it carefully so that something is always flowering from April to October. When she points out particular flowers the names enchant me. Sweet William, creeping phlox, delphiniums, black-eyed Susans, pinks, bearded irises, cosmos. In between the blooms she has planted clumps of parsley and basil and oregano. This is her sole concession to being practical. She likes to cook with fresh herbs. Behind some lilac impatiens are two clumps of chives, and later in the summer pinkish mauve pom-poms will wave from the tops of their tall narrow stems.

I read a Chinese proverb somewhere: "If you have two coins buy bread with one and daffodils with the other, for bread feeds the body but daffodils feed the soul."

When I am with Fiona, I am often reminded that I have a soul. I can't say how it happens, and yet I know we would agree if we turned our conversation to philosophies of life and the reasons for human existence. We would surely agree that the reason our mothers give birth to us and the reason we populate this earth is not to accumulate possessions or acquire riches or assume power over the lives of others. We are here to be with each other. What other reason could there be than to share our pleasures and sorrows, to hold and be held, to tend the small hurts and the large ones, to celebrate together, to seek each other out with gentle hearts and open minds and loving hands.

That night, full to the brim with delicious food, we sat side by side on her sofa, which is covered in a worn fabric that can only be described as flowerful. And it occurred to me that we are here to be true and loyal to each other all our lives. I wished the bowl of lilies of the valley and forget-me-nots was on the coffee table before us, so I could look at the tiny flowers and relish their wild loveliness. Sitting there, smelling the lilies of the valley from the next room, I knew as well as I know my own name that our reason for being here is not only to live with compassion for one another for as many years as we have in this world but also to honour our planet as much as we honour our selves.

It was one of those rare moments when everything in my life seemed so simple and clear.

That moment passed and, once again, with it went my urge to express my love by touching her. But later, the memory of those moments nudged an afterthought. I had inhibited myself. I had withheld myself from her. That is not how I want to be. I imagine my perfect self as always knowing and being true to my feelings. I wish I could trust my impulses and act on them.

I never expected to feel safe with a woman who lives with a man. There is something about a man that strains a woman. But not Fiona. She is not strained. Fiona is not like other women.

Our relationship was not always this way. Last year, after her forty-fifth birthday party, I withdrew from her and refused to acknowledge her when we met, except in a coldly polite fashion. It was my fault, my choice, although it did not feel like a choice.

I knew she wished to renew our friendship, yet I turned away for reasons I only dimly understand. Reasons that have nothing to do with her and me, and more to do with the behaviour I learned as a young child: to mask my emotions and to be untrue to myself.

I have tried to dissect that shameful time. I have gone back over it many times, taking apart each moment, every scene, and still it does not make sense. I wonder if I was jealous. Could it be that simple? Not that jealousy is a simple emotion. It does not make sense, that I would feel jealous of Fiona. What is there between us to inspire envy or mistrust? We are loyal in our friendship. Yet I felt betrayed.

When it was over and we were friends again, I gave her a book. *The Fountain Overflows* by Rebecca West. I found a first edition, published in 1956, in a second-hand book store near where I work.

I read the book first and liked it, not just the story but also the thick cream-coloured pages and the expert binding which meant the pages would never come loose and fall out. I considered keeping it for myself but decided to give it to Fiona. Presenting the book to her would give me pleasure, and I was sure my feelings of regret and loss would be brief.

I hoped she would enjoy Rebecca West's writing. She likes British Literature. This is something we share, girlhoods of reading Jane Austen and Charlotte Brontë. In school we read Shakespeare and Dickens and Hemingway and at home we read the women, on our own time.

I hoped Fiona would also like the book because the

children in it play piano. The main character is a talented pianist, with humorous and set opinions on music and musical ability (or the lack of it) in others.

Fiona plays the piano. Someone at her birthday party told me she is a skilled musician. I can't tell. One piano player is much like the other, as far as I'm concerned.

I yearn to sit down and make music whenever I see a piano. When I was eleven I begged my mother to let me take lessons. She said no, adamantly no, although I kept nagging her. Eventually she said, "There's no point in it. It would be hard work and you never finish anything you start. It would be a waste of perfectly good money." The following Christmas she gave me an acoustic guitar and a book on how to teach yourself to play. I was astonished and wondered how she could have misunderstood.

Years later I realized she did not have the money to buy a piano or pay for weekly lessons.

When I gave Fiona the book, I told her about my youthful desire to play the piano. For a moment I thought she was going to hug me. She cradled the book to her breasts.

David was there, the night of her birthday party. I went, knowing he would be there but wanting to be there too. I was determined to celebrate with her. I don't think he likes me but I don't care. I rarely see him. He works long hours at his office, sometimes into the night. When we meet at her house he is never there, although usually we meet on neutral ground in a restaurant.

No matter how liberal straight people are, and I have been surprised by how many are, the word *lesbian* has an aura of danger and wickedness for them. I know Fiona has brought me out to David. I can tell by the way he talks to me and the way he looks at me. I have noticed that non-lesbian women have a tendency to do this, to bring me out to their companions and to their friends and co-workers.

I tried to ignore him, just as I ignored the other men at her party. I don't believe my behaviour was rude. Straight men routinely ignore women at parties. They prefer to talk to one another, except when they want to flirt with one of us.

But when I went into the kitchen to get myself a drink, I couldn't ignore his arm around Fiona's shoulders. I stood there for a moment, unable to move, feeling like someone had punched me in the stomach.

I left the party early. When I got home I found I could not get to sleep. In the wee hours of the morning I wanted to talk to her. But how could I phone her, with him there beside her in bed? He might answer the phone. He might ask her, Why does she call you in the middle of the night? He might say, Why do you hang around with a *lesbian?* At some point during the night I decided to end our friendship. I didn't want to feel so awful. I didn't know what I felt except I never wanted to see her again.

I missed her more than I ever imagined possible.

Fiona eventually ended our estrangement. She called me and insisted we meet somewhere to talk. We agreed on a trendy eatery on Elgin Street.

I was so nervous I couldn't look at her across the table.

She asked, "What on earth is wrong? Please tell me. What's going on?"

I wanted to speak the truth.

"I don't know exactly. You live in such a straight world and I don't feel part of it. I don't want to be part of it, don't mistake me, but we live so differently. You see," I said, staring into my black coffee, "our lifestyles have nothing in common. If I want to be at your birthday party, I have to be in a room with all these straight couples and I have nothing in common with them, especially the men, and it makes me wonder what I have in common with you."

She rested her hands on the table, palms up. "You complain that other people aren't very liberal, but perhaps you are not very liberal. Is that it?"

"No! I knew you wouldn't understand. Heterosexuality is the accepted way of life. Nobody has to be liberal about it. It is the way we are expected to be, don't you see? No, you can't understand, can you, because you are straight." I hoped she would deny it, would say she wasn't straight, would say she understood perfectly what I meant. I looked at her.

She drew her eyebrows together as she spoke. "It sounds like you are condemning me because I'm straight. That's not fair."

I looked around at the other people in the restaurant. The word *straight* sounded so peculiar from her mouth. It obviously wasn't a word she used much. She had no need to think or speak of herself as straight. Is it her fault that straightness is not an issue? But I wished she would work a little harder at understanding what it is like for me. Nobody goes around whispering behind her back, Did you know that Fiona's *straight?*

"I'm sorry," I said, feeling great sorrow. And then I lied before I spoke the truth again. "I didn't want to hurt you. I don't know what happened, except I know I felt hurt and then I hurt you. You see, I've never had a friendship with a

straight woman. Not like this. My friends are all dykes."
As soon as I said it I knew it was true and that a friendship
with a straight woman was different. I would have to
think about that. "I have missed you," I admitted.
  She smiled, at last. "I've missed you, too."
  Soon we talked of other things.
  It was a small incident, an almost nothingness in the
scheme of things. One flaw in three years. Yet I can't forget
it. I hate myself for my behaviour and I wish my emotions
were clear to me. I wish I could recognize what I felt,
could know precisely what happened and understand
myself and explain everything to her. To not know what I
feel or why I feel it is surely a pathetic state.
  I gave her *The Fountain Overflows* a month later, on an
evening when we met at her house for supper. Days after I
gave her the book, it occurred to me that I should have
given her a lesbian book. *Somebody Should Kiss You* by
Brenda Brooks or *Scuttlebutt* by Jana Williams or a collection of stories by lesbians such as *Tide Lines*. Instead, I had
abetted her straightness by giving her a straight book
written by a straight woman.
  I decided I would give her a lesbian book for Christmas, which was still many months away.
  We rarely talk about my writing. I can't say why. She
never asks and I am too shy to impose myself, although
my writing is more important to me than anything. I have
never told her that. It would sound so dramatic and self-
centred to say it like that.
  This evening she wears black. Black leather trousers
and black silk t-shirt and black beads on the silver hoops
she wears in her ears.
  I move a little closer to her, bending across the café

table to get a better view of the photographs she has brought from her forty-fifth birthday party. It was almost a year ago and I had forgotten that pictures were taken.

"I like this one," she says, laughing and looking at me over the top of her half glasses. "Look at us. I think it captures the mood, don't you? They all turned out, which is nothing short of a miracle with my camera."

I wonder if she means it is a miracle because he took the picture. She would never say that, would never criticize another person. It is so like her, to blame the camera rather than the photographer. This is something I love about her: she accepts people. So often I feel like I am a mean woman because I am critical and inclined to judge.

I reach for the photograph. There we are, together on her sofa, our mouths open with laughter. She told him to take the picture. He had been photographing other guests and she called out to him. "David! Take one of us." And she threw her right arm over my shoulders.

She waits patiently while I study the picture. "Usually I have my eyes closed when the shutter opens," she said. "It seems to be an automatic reflex. Point a camera at me and I blink." She blinks three times while chuckling at herself.

"It's a good picture of you." I hand the photograph back to her. "May I have a copy?" I don't have any pictures of her.

She takes it from me and glances at it. "Yes, of course." She adds it to the top of the pile and moves the photographs to the other side of her cup.

We sit in this café talking about flowers. Her knowledge is much greater than mine. Her voice lifts and spins. I watch her talk and imagine her at home, sitting on the flowerful sofa, with her glasses balanced midway down her nose as she leafs through garden books and plans additions to the wide bed of earth against the back fence.

Does she think of me when we are not together?

"I've planted blue lobelia," she says, pulling at the silver hoop in her left ear. "Have you ever seen it?" I shake my head. "I wish I'd pointed it out to you when you were over for supper. I love the wild look of it." She sips gingerly from her cup of hot café au lait and then licks the foam from her upper lip. "It's more like a weed than a cultivated plant. The flowers have a touch of white inside."

I remember dinner at her house and the dark lines under her nails and I can almost smell the lilies of the valley. Again, I want to reach out and touch her hand.

The dirt was under nails that are as broad as they are long. My mother, who reads palms, says large nails are a sign of a generous nature. My nails, she said when I asked, are fairly large and the slight outward flare of my thumb means I have some flexibility. Only some. My mother prefers to read the hands of strangers. Someday I must ask her to read Fiona's hand. She has never met Fiona.

My mother says it is all there, in the hand, if you know how to read.

Fiona's hands straighten the pile of photographs and move them to the other side of the table. Her nails are clean tonight. "I don't know why it's called blue when it's really purple. It is a colour unlike any other. So deep and rich. I must show it to you."

I could listen to her forever. But I am also selfish. I want to tell her about me. "I saw a movie last night. Have you seen *Steel Magnolias?*"

"No. I remember reading a review when it came out. I

think it won some awards."

"You must see it. It's a thought-provoking film. I'll see it again, if you want to see it."

I stir sugar into my café au lait and look up in time to see two women walk arm-in-arm past the window. Precious strangers. I smile. The taller woman smiles back. Fiona does not notice. She is dipping into her foam and sipping it from the spoon.

I don't tell her I cried, sitting alone in the Mayfair Theatre. I wiped away the tears with the back of my hand. I didn't have any tissue with me because I never cry at movies.

The Mayfair is a bargain movie theatre. They offer two movies for the price of one every night of the week. But I didn't stay for the second feature. I walked home, sniffing occasionally, and thinking about the movie that had made me cry in public.

When I watched *Steel Magnolias* I felt the agony of motherhood, all the hopes and dreams mothers have for children. It made me wonder what agonies my mother has endured. What dreams did she have for me? Does she still worry about me? Do I disappoint her?

The movie is also about the nurturing kind of love I find among women. And about how men abdicate real responsibility, except sometimes financial, for women and children. It shows, better than any film I have seen, the emptiness of the word 'masculinity.' Manliness is surely an image created by men so they can deceive each other and pretend strength over women.

Can I say that to Fiona? Or will she feel she must defend David and her male co-workers?

Fiona and I love movies. Sometimes we spend hours

talking about the ones we have liked and those we didn't like, discussing the plot and characters and the cinematography. We usually agree. From time to time one of us rents a video and we watch it at her house, because she has a VCR.

We abhor unnecessary violence. We avoid those movies that are filled with guns and knives and fist fights and bombs and car chases. The ones, and there are so many of them, that display all the hysterical savageness of men. I am proud to say I have never seen a Rambo movie.

I have noticed that critics and censors are preoccupied with sex, which they call making love, but mostly ignore violence. Journalists interview actors about what it is like doing love scenes and the actors invariably go on about how difficult it is. It is not romantic, each one insists. It is uncomfortable and more embarrassing than anything to do *that* surrounded by cameras and a film crew. When I see the movie I am always disappointed because the love scene has so little to do with love.

No one ever asks the actor what it feels like to punch another actor, to slap, to shoot, to knife, to strangle, to rape.

Fiona pulls out her calendar. "How about next Thursday? I'll get it and we can watch it at my house." She looks at me over the top of her glasses, waiting for my response. "Let's order pizza for a change. And I'll make popcorn during the movie. How does that sound?"

Will I cry when I see it a second time? How will I feel if I cry in front of her? Will she cry?

Fiona and I never talk about sex. We talk about so many things, but somehow we never get around to sex. It may be me, my reticence that stops us. I don't want to hear about him and because of him I don't want to talk about what it's like to love a woman.

I sense that she doesn't want to talk about David either. She only mentions him casually from time to time. I don't know if she loves him passionately or if she daydreams about leaving him. He is a mystery to me. Occasionally she'll say something like, "I went to a play with David last night," or "We're going to paint the bathroom this weekend."

Sometimes we talk about work, her job, my job. We worked together for a year, until she left to take another job. She was my boss for that year, although I never thought of her as my boss. She is not bossy.

I never expected to have a friendship with someone I work with. I have always tried to keep work separate from the rest of my life. Fiona was the exception. During that year we spent time together each working day. We were together more than I am with my family or other friends. At least once a week we would go out for lunch. We took turns paying. We never got back to work in less than two hours.

She always looked smart at work. Even on the days when she came in wearing blue jeans. She is unique. We all are, but she expresses her specialness in the way she dresses. She does not dress like many professional women, in skirts and matching jackets or smart business dresses. Her feet are never crammed into pointed high-heel shoes. She wears trousers more often than not, trousers of deep purple silk or geometrically-patterned cotton in blues and greens. She wears practical shoes, always flat and often fancy.

She has been wearing the same pair of glasses for three

years, half-glasses for reading. They sit down her nose and look as if they'll slide off at any minute. But they never do.

"What time shall I come over?"

"Around six thirty? We'll have the pizza first and then watch the movie. David will be away at a conference in Victoria." She writes in the calendar. "And I want to remember to show you the lobelia. Remind me, if I forget." She puts the book and the photographs away in her bag and pulls out a folded paper. "Do you remember I told you I'm going to a cottage in July? Would you like to come up for a weekend, the one after the long weekend? There won't be anyone around except us. We can swim all day and eat all evening. I drew a map for you, with a great deal of detail so that you can't get lost even if you try." She hands me the paper. "You'll come, won't you?"

I nod as I take the map and fold it in a tidy package and stuff it into the pocket of my jeans. I can't imagine myself saying no to her.

Her fingers fiddle nervously with the spoon, then with the torn and empty sugar packets. Why is she fidgeting? She is usually so calm.

I look at her eyes above the glasses. "Can I bring anything," I ask politely.

"Just yourself. And your bathing suit." Fiona folds an empty sugar packet in half and then in half again. She looks up at me. "You could come for the whole week, if you like."

I watch her fingers tuck the folded sugar packets under her saucer and then she reaches for a full packet.

"That sounds like fun. I'll see what I can arrange at work. You used to let me take my holidays whenever I wanted, but things have changed since you left." I study the top of our table, feeling excited or nervous or something, feeling jittery at the thought of spending days and nights alone with her. But if I spend a whole week with her, I'll lose a week of work on my novel. It is so difficult to find enough time for it and it desperately needs work. It is two hundred pages of awkwardness and some chaos. Perhaps I could borrow a portable computer and work at her cottage in the mornings? Do I know anyone who has a lap-top?

And then I notice that she isn't wearing her wedding band. When did she stop wearing it? Why did she take it off? Surely I would have noticed if her finger was bare the evening she had dirt under her nails.

Does it mean anything? Dare I ask her?

"Fiona, why aren't you wearing your wedding band?"

She looks at her left hand and then at me.

"I need to talk to you but I don't feel ready to talk yet. Maybe I will by Thursday. I need to think things through a little more . . . "

Aprons and Homemade Bread

t is a lazy summer morning. I can hear the birds chattering in the trees. Bev has gone to her waged work, leaving us with the after-breakfast kitchen mess. The sun shines in through the kitchen window. Your soft head is lying against my shoulder and your fine blonde hair tickles my jaw. We are content.

You drool and my shirt has a wet patch, an amazing round wet spot over my left breast, and my nipple feels the seeping dampness. This was a freshly-laundered shirt when I put it on an hour ago. Your left hand grips a fistful of my shirt and skin. Tightly, you hold onto my chest. Sitting on my leg, leaning against my arm, you drool again and grab at the paper as I try to write.

I smell of baby vomit, regurgitated 2% milk. Bev says you must have a slight allergy to milk. I secretly wonder if it's tension that upsets your stomach. We have our share of anxiety. Some days my stomach aches and I hate the thought of cooking, can barely tolerate the smell or sight of food.

The doorbell rings and startles us. There now, sshhh, I say, as I put you in the high chair.

It is the landowner. Greedy, a bully with greasy yellow-grey hair and filthy fingernails, his nervous eyes constantly peer past me as he complains and yells. He insists on coming in to inspect the house. I refuse. He thinks he can intimidate us. Finally he leaves, and I slam the door shut.

You're crying. You don't like loud noises. Neither do I. I wish you wouldn't cry. I never know precisely what to do for you. Carrying you in my body for nine months has not made me an expert. Bev has never been pregnant and she knows more about your needs than I do. Don't cry, please don't cry. There there now, sshhh, don't cry, there, there, sshhhhh. I pick you up abruptly, roughly. My hands lift your body from the high chair and your head jerks backwards. You're so surprised that you stop crying, then you regain your composure and continue to cry.

I carry you upstairs, There now, sshhh, to our bedroom, and you sob against my shoulder. I place you on a blanket on the floor and I curl up on the bed. You look up at me and shove a baby fistful of bedclothes into your mouth. Are you hungry? Or are you consoling yourself? I feel so alone with you. Mother and child. Isn't it touching. Sometimes I think it is, when I am feeling loving with you. Other times I feel the horror of this total responsibility. How often and in what ways do you suffer because of my power and my powerlessness? What do I teach you of power? You smile at me. What do I teach you of love? You are dependent on me, my whims, my moods, yet you smile at me. O sweetheart, it's time to feed you, change you, do the breakfast dishes while you snooze in the high chair.

While I am drying the dishes, the doorbell startles us a second time. You wake, crying. There now. Sshhh.

It is Sandra. I give her decaffeinated coffee and hold you as she tells me about last weekend. She went to a trendy bar and her lover, Mandy, hit a man because he kept bothering them. The man grabbed Mandy in a head-lock and smashed his fist into her delicate face. Sandra is distraught. I stood there, she tells me. I stood there. He hit her again and again. Nobody tried to stop him. I just stood there.

I have already heard about what happened to Mandy. Everybody's talking about it. One woman said Mandy shouldn't have hit him because violence never solves any-thing. Another said Mandy shouldn't have hit him unless she was ready to fight, she should have been prepared for his violent response. Another woman said Mandy should have left the bar, that Mandy and Sandra were asking for trouble by going to a place that straights go. And another said we should get together, a gang of women, and go after him and beat him up, because if he's allowed to get away with it this time he'll beat other women.

I don't know what Mandy should or shouldn't have done. She has made me think about violence. I wonder where she got the nerve to hit him. Could I make my hand into a fist and punch someone? What would I do in a violent confrontation? I try, but fail, to imagine a fist punching my face.

I don't know what to say. I tell Sandra that I know nothing about violence, that I have escaped violence so far in my life. This is not entirely true.

When I was married to a man, he used to show me how he could hold me down, pin me to the floor, immobile and helpless. I struggled to get free while he laughed. He was just being playful, just having fun, he said. He got angry the time I kicked him accidently and hurt him as I thrashed around in a panic.

Once he shoved me against a closed door. He wasn't feeling playful that day. Another time he threw a bottle of beer at the kitchen wall, beside my head. Afterwards, I cleaned up the mess. Once, when I insisted he move out immediately, he slapped me on the face — and moved out a few days later. I felt each assault was my fault. Yet I closed my heart to him. Passive resistance.

I remember the time we talked about rape. He told me not to resist a rapist. Never, he said. You won't stand a chance against any man.

I said, I'll kick him in the balls.

No! Don't do that, he said. Whatever you do, don't do that. You'll only make him madder and then he'll *really* hurt you. Don't do anything.

Now I know he was wrong. He was protecting his own precious balls. He fed into my weakness to hide his own. He wanted me to believe his anger and his violence were my responsibility, my fault. He wanted a passive victim.

Men are threatened when we stop being passive victims, I tell Sandra. They get crazy, go berserk, become hysterical. I tell her about the time Bev took a self-defence course for women. A few weeks later, she and her then-husband were fighting with words and he picked up a knife because he believed she would be able to defend herself now so he needed help, a knife, to intimidate and overpower her. Just by taking the course she had ceased to be a passive victim in his eyes.

Sandra starts to cry and I put my arms around her. I was passive, she sobs. Her tears leave large wet spots on the shoulder of my shirt. I give her more coffee, and she cuddles you. He's so tiny, she says, as she strokes your soft blonde hair. We have lunch, the three of us, then Sandra leaves, and you take a nap.

I have two hours to myself, to write. But before I start writing the phone rings.

It's my sister. I tell her about Sandra's visit and Mandy's encounter at the trendy bar. Thanks to Mandy, the subject of violence is becoming everyday conversation.

My sister starts talking. She tells me that her husband threatens her, punches her, throws her around. Her two small children watch as their father tries to destroy her. She speaks calmly and I listen politely.

I don't know what to say. I talk to her about the frustrations of surviving in this world. Men are encouraged to express anger, to be violent and destructive. I hold my emotions inward and intellectualize. I can't quite believe we are having this conversation. I hear you crying and it is a relief to have an excuse to say goodbye to my sister.

Words leave me as anger fills me up. I have never liked her husband. Now I feel a violent hatred toward him.

You are wet, so I change you. We sit and cuddle while you suck at a bottle of 2% milk. This afternoon is wasted. You want my attention and I can't concentrate to write.

As I prepare supper, I remember the time my sister had a huge bruise on her face. I believed her when she said she'd fallen into a door knob. Although I wondered at the time how on earth someone falls into a door knob. I noticed that she made a point of explaining the bruise to everyone, but I accepted her explanation at face value.

When Bev comes home, we are sitting on the kitchen floor, you and I, making music, tapping on the vinyl tiles with teaspoons. She kisses you first, and you laugh and drool all over her trousers. She kisses me second and hugs me. I hold onto her as if my life depends on her. She doesn't mention the piles of dirty dishes.

When I tell her about my sister, as we eat supper, she sighs at least three times before she says, Domestic violence is surely more common than the flu.

The word *domestic* makes me think of jars of strawberry jam, aprons, homemade bread, clothes hanging on the line.

What's your sister going to do?

She wants to leave him and take the children, I reply. But she doesn't have a job or any money or a place to go. Then I tell her about Sandra's visit.

Bev starts to clear the dishes from the table. You've had quite a day.

I say, And the landowner was here again this morning.

You start talking to Bev, in that strange language you are inventing. When she doesn't talk back, as she usually does, you start to cry. She stands at the sink, staring at the piles of dishes. I pick you up. You cry louder. Slow tears slide down my cheeks and drop onto your fine blonde hair. Bev comes over and puts her arms around both of us.

Sshhh, she says, Never mind. It'll be alright.

Later, when Bev and I are sitting in the living room, and you are asleep in your crib upstairs, and I am tuning my guitar, and Bev is reading a novel, she looks up and says, Men are such violent bastards!

I think about that, when we're in bed, me curled against Bev's warm back. I remember the time, long before you were born, when I almost hit a woman. We had been lovers, this woman and I, but she got secretly involved with someone else. I had been trying to get hold of her for eighteen hours. She was evading me and I was not accepting of her wish to avoid me. I couldn't sleep, couldn't eat. I wanted to see her, wanted to know what was going on. When she finally answered her phone, my hands trembled. I rushed to her apartment, running most of the way.

I arrived, out of breath, and felt warm for the first time in days. I stood before her and all I could see was the noise in my head. My arm was in the air, ready to strike. It was as if I was standing apart, watching myself. As my arm came downward I stopped the movement and my selves came together. The noise changed to silence. I collapsed, crying.

I don't want to be violent. I don't want you to be violent, either. Ever.

I will remind Bev, in the morning, that women are violent too. I have learned to be violent, and I teach you what I have learned. What can I do about it?

Bev, I say quietly so I won't wake you, Are you asleep?

Yes, she says.

Bev, how come all this violence is here now?

She turns over to face me. In the darkness I can see her eyes, her nose, the movement of her mouth. It just happened. Things happen in cycles. Everything is connected. Violence breeds violence. Conversations about violence breed conversations about violence.

I turn over and Bev curls against my back. I'll phone my sister in the morning and invite her for lunch, her and

my two nieces, your cousins. I don't know what to say to
her. Could she stay here with the children for a while?
Domestic violence. I must get to sleep. You'll be up at
six, won't you, wanting a bottle of 2% milk and pureed
bananas.

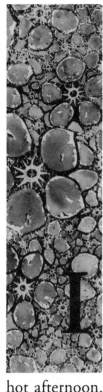

Threads

sabelle knew something was wrong the moment she stepped off the yellow school bus. She could hear music from across the fields, shocking the muggy stillness of the hot afternoon.

She turned and waved goodbye to her best friend, Betty, then walked slowly toward the white frame house — dragging her feet along the dirt road and sending up small clouds of dust. It was a bad sign when her mother played loud music. It wasn't worth Isabelle's life to speak to her, to ask her when supper would be ready or to tell her she needed help with homework. She'd either snap at Isabelle or pretend she hadn't heard.

Isabelle stood outside the back door for a few minutes, wondering what to do. Patsy Cline was singing *Crazy.* The music was loud, so loud Isabelle could barely hear herself think. She had to go in, but she didn't want to. What had upset her mother?

The song ended and there was silence. Isabelle shifted her books from one arm to the other and waited a little longer before walking into the kitchen. Her mother was standing at the sink, peeling potatoes. Isabelle looked at her quickly, then down at her dusty shoes.

Without turning around, her mother asked, "How was school?"

"It was okay." Isabelle glanced at her mother again and then walked across the immaculate linoleum floor and upstairs to her room, to keep out of her mother's way. Whatever was wrong, she would stay in her room until it passed. She hoped it would pass soon.

Isabelle lay across her bed, the math book open beside her. The last time it happened was a few weeks ago on a Saturday morning. Her mother wanted to go into town to get some groceries and material to start a new quilt. Her father said he needed the truck. He had an order for firewood and it had to be delivered today because the guy had been waiting for a few weeks. And after that, though he didn't say so, he needed the truck because he was going fishing. Isabelle knew, and her mother knew, because he had sat in the kitchen the evening before going through his tackle box. And they both knew that nobody needed firewood urgently in May. Her mother was so angry she didn't speak to him for three days, not one word, and when she spoke to Isabelle the sentences were brief and stiff.

Isabelle sat up and balanced the math book on her lap. Everything had been fine when she left for school this morning. Had something happened when her father came in for lunch?

She heard him downstairs. He let the screen door slam shut, as he always did, and then she heard him talking to her mother. If this was her father's fault, he didn't seem to know it.

Once they were sitting down for supper, her mother said, "A reporter from Ottawa phoned this afternoon."

Isabelle and her father looked at her.

Her father said, "A reporter? What for? What did he want? Why did he phone?"

Her mother shrugged. "Don't ask me." She screwed the lid on the jar of dill pickles and thumped it down on the table. "It's a lady. She said she wants to talk about my quilts. She'll be here after supper."

Her mother was talking to her father. She was even volunteering information. Then what was wrong? It didn't make any sense.

Isabelle propped her elbow on the table and rested her head on her hand. How exciting! A reporter was coming here, to their house, to talk to her mother. Isabelle wanted to ask so many questions. Why was the reporter coming? When would she be here? Why was she interested in quilts?

She was a woman. Isabelle had never thought about it before, but now that she did she realized the news on TV was done by men. Wasn't that weird. Could women be reporters?

But Isabelle said nothing and asked nothing. Her mother was unpredictable when she was in one of her moods and no one was safe. The most innocent question, any casual statement, and Isabelle could be ordered from the table and sent to her room for the evening.

Isabelle wanted to understand what was happening.

This was exciting. Nothing like it had ever happened before. A reporter coming to their house. Surely her mother should be pleased and flattered?

Her father left while Isabelle was clearing away the supper dishes, saying he had to fix the hitch on the tractor. Isabelle knew that was an excuse. He always watched the news after supper and drank a cup of coffee, before going back out to work. He wanted to keep out of her mother's way too.

Her mother put the leftover mashed potatoes in the fridge and wiped off the table before going upstairs. She stayed there for more than an hour.

Isabelle washed and dried the dishes and swept the kitchen floor, for once not having to be asked to do it. If she was good maybe her mother's mood would pass. She opened a bottle of Coke, carefully putting the cap in the garbage pail, and returned the opener to its place in the drawer. Had this reporter said something to upset her mother?

She went upstairs to her room to get her history book, walking quietly, trying to be invisible. She settled herself at the kitchen table with the bottle of Coke and her history book, but her mind was too busy to heed the words on the pages. Who cared about Elizabeth the Virgin Queen or Mary, Queen of Scots when a reporter was coming to her house.

Her mother came back downstairs wearing her best dress, the pretty green one she had ordered from the catalogue last summer, and lipstick and her pearl screw-on earrings and sheer stockings and black high heel sandals. She looked so beautiful, sitting on the sofa, staring into space while she listened to Pasty Cline on the hi-fi.

Isabelle sat at the kitchen table, pretending to read her history book. She could smell her mother's perfume, *Je Reviens*. Her mother was acting like this was a special occasion, all dressed up as if she was going to church or to a party.

She was even more puzzled by her mother's behaviour when the reporter arrived. Her mother jumped up at the sound of the car and walked quickly to the door. She tripped as she stepped off the porch to greet the woman and, regaining her balance, blurted out, "Why do you want to talk to me?"

Her mother wasn't like that. Her mother was graceful and tactful, and always polite with strangers. Isabelle pressed her face against the screen door as she strained to hear every word.

"Mrs. Buchanan?" The reporter extended her right hand. As they shook hands, she said, "My editor saw one of your quilts somewhere last year. I think it was the Carp fair. He keeps a file of ideas for stories and he was going through it and decided this would make a good story for the women's page. Women like to read about other women. And we have many readers out here in the Valley."

Her mother and the reporter sat in the living room, one at either end of the sofa, sipping tea from her mother's good china cups after stirring milk into the tea with small silver-plated teaspoons that were usually kept in the silver-ware chest. Isabelle perched on the edge of a footstool, close to the doorway. She was silent throughout the interview. She didn't want to draw attention to herself, in case her mother noticed and ordered her out of the room. Her left hand played with her hair, twisting it around and around her fingers until she remembered her mother hated when she did that. She held her left hand with the right one in her lap.

The reporter asked a lot of questions and made notes on a pad.

Where did you learn to quilt?

Did your mother quilt? Your grandmother?

How long does it take to make a quilt?

Do you sell them? How much do you get for them?

What do you do with the money?

Where have your quilts been displayed? Have you won any prizes?

Do you have any other hobbies?

Does your daughter quilt?

Isabelle was relieved when her mother said, "No, Isabelle doesn't quilt. She's not much for sewing," and didn't reveal to the reporter that she had tried repeatedly to teach Isabelle to sew and before she finally gave up she had been known to mutter that Isabelle's stitches looked like the drunken tracks of a wounded bird.

It was an hour of revelations for Isabelle. She had never heard her mother talk about the quilts before. It was just something her mother did, like all the other things she did around the house. One quilt was displayed each fall at the country fair, as her mother explained to the reporter, but that was nothing compared to Mrs. Muchmore in Pakenham. She got an award from the Governor General for organizing the fair. Mrs. Muchmore's picture had been in both Ottawa newspapers and the local paper and on the TV news. People still talked about it.

Her mother went upstairs and returned a moment later carrying three quilts.

Isabelle watched her mother spread the white and pale blue quilt across the kitchen table and dared to move closer and stand beside her mother. This was the quilt from her bed.

"I was planning on a bright blue for the background here, the sky. Something bright and cheerful was what I had in mind. But when I got to the store, this shade caught my eye." Her mother's hand stroked the pacific blue cotton. "I made this quilt for Isabelle. The clouds moving across the sky are to remind her that everything moves and changes and nothing ever stays the same."

Her mother was relaxed now, smiling and more like herself. But not entirely herself. She was saying things Isabelle had never heard before.

Isabelle's left hand worried a fistful of hair as she listened. She hadn't known that her mother deliberately put clouds on the quilt, hadn't known there was a reason for the design, and hadn't realized her mother made the quilt especially for her. It lay on Isabelle's bed. But that was because her mother had cut the mauve chenille bedspread into pieces, saying it was old and shabby and she couldn't bear to look at it for one more minute and it was only good for rags. That same evening her mother had replaced the bedspread with her latest quilt and stood in the doorway of Isabelle's bedroom, looking at it for the longest time. Isabelle wondered at the fuss. It was just a quilt.

"Sometimes I use the traditional patterns like Log Cabin or Double Irish Chain. I like scrape quilts, too," her mother explained, "or sometimes I make the design from something I see. One of my favourites was a tall blue spruce standing in a clump of snow, surrounded by smaller trees, with snow on the branches. You know how trees look after a snowfall? And for my sister-in-law's baby I made a quilt of animals. All different animals. Dogs and pigs and bears and horses and sheep. They're wearing costumes and dancing. The bears, they were my favourite, are doing somersaults."

The reporter photographed Isabelle and her mother with the quilt, each holding a corner and smiling at the camera. Isabelle was so excited at the thought of having her picture in the paper that she wanted to cry. She couldn't wait until she got to school in the morning to tell everyone. Her friends weren't going to believe this.

Maybe she would become a reporter. It didn't seem like a difficult job. Just asking questions and writing down the answers. Would she have to go to university and live in the city? Would she have to buy a camera and learn how to use it? She'd ask her mother later, when things were back to normal.

The photograph was in the paper the following Saturday. Her father drove into town and bought five copies and gave one to Isabelle. The caption beneath the photo read, "Mrs. Buchanan (left) with quilt made for daughter Isabelle, aged fifteen."

Isabelle's mother carefully cut the photograph and article out of the paper, using her good sewing scissors, the ones she kept in a basket in the closet. She bought a frame with glass in it, at the five-and-dime store in town, and hung the photograph in the kitchen over the sink. She never brought it to anyone's attention, but if a visitor mentioned the framed picture she would take the article from the top drawer of the sideboard and pass it around.

Isabelle borrowed her mother's good scissors to cut the article and photograph from her newspaper. She placed the clipping carefully in the front of her geography book and carried it to school where she taped it inside her locker door. Her friends stood around, asking questions and chattering excitedly. It was the main topic of conversation between classes for almost a week, until Thursday when Betty was invited to be a bridesmaid at her cousin's wedding and all talk turned to marriage.

The newspaper photograph gave Isabelle a tiny jittery feeling in her stomach every time she opened her locker door. She got the same feeling at home when she looked at the framed picture while washing dishes. Now that she knew her mother had made the quilt especially for her, she cherished it. She stopped lounging on the bed and lay on the floor beside her bed or sat at the kitchen table to do her homework.

Sometimes at night, before she fell asleep, Isabelle would think about the clouds on the quilt and that her mother had made it especially for her and she would feel like leaping out of bed and dancing around the room.

She kept these feelings to herself.

Scots Pine and Cranberry Chains

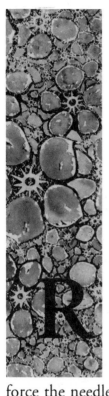osa is afraid to speak the thoughts in her head. Anxiety, tight and painful like a clenched fist, sits in her stomach.

The next berry is hard and Rosa has to force the needle through, jabbing herself in the process. She sucks her sore finger and thinks, I have to tell her. But how can I say what I am thinking in such a way that she won't take offence? How can I get her to listen? How can I get her to understand my feelings, without the conversation turning into a quarrel?

"You're taking a long time with those berries."

Rosa looks up, her finger still in her mouth. Maud is frowning and standing back from the tree to study the arrangement of lights.

Rosa loathes the fear in herself. She removes the finger from her mouth and examines the sore.

"I'm thinking," she says, hoping Maud will ask her

what she is thinking about.

"Yeah, well, I'm just about ready to put the cranberries on the tree. Could you think a little faster."

Rosa hears the command behind the words. The fist in her stomach grows and tightens at the same time. She is trying to think of a tactful way to tell Maud their relationship is a fraud. She wants to say to her, We are impostors. We are liars. We pretend and pretend until we don't know what's real any more and, worst of all, we deceive ourselves.

Rosa takes a cigarette from the pack on the coffee table and lights it with an inch-high flame from an orange lighter. Maud feels no need for tact when she speaks. Rosa wonders, not for the first time, if Maud's forthright approach is more honest. It seems more effective.

She inhales deeply and watches Maud attach a row of lights to the branches. Each detail is important to Maud, from the shape of the carefully chosen tree to the arrangement of hanging white balls. Maud insists on buying a Scots pine. Rosa can't remember why it has to be a Scots pine, although each year they drive around to Christmas tree lots searching for the ideal one at a bargain price. Maud never looks at the spruce trees or the balsams. There is never any discussion, except about whether or not a particular Scots pine is really worth twenty-five or thirty dollars.

Their first year together, Rosa protested. They were standing in the parking lot of a shopping centre, surrounded by evergreens of every shape and size. Rosa's fingers were stiff from the frosty December cold and she was hungry.

She had said, somewhat impatiently, "It's sinful to buy

a tree and a week or two later turn it into garbage."

Maud pulled a frozen Scots pine to an upright position. "What do you think of this one? Did he say everything in this row is twenty dollars?" She looked over her right shoulder at Rosa. "Will you hold it so I can see how it looks?"

Rosa took hold of the tree trunk and Maud stood back.

"These conifers are grown specifically for the Christmas market."

Rosa said, "That may be . . . " but Maud interrupted her.

"There are farmers who plant trees especially for Christmas. It's how they make their living. We're not destroying any natural resources or harming the environment by buying one because the trees come from Christmas-tree farms and when they cut the trees they replant. If we don't buy them, the farmers will lose their income."

Rosa chewed the corner of her lip as she helped Maud carry the tree to the car. She was not entirely convinced.

Rosa exhales a cloud of grey smoke and looks at the tree Maud picked this year. When she was growing up, her mother used to say that Rosa only remembered what she chose to remember. Her mother would sigh, a small sigh filled with reproach, and mutter about Rosa's selective memory.

She wants to remember why Maud insists they buy a Scots pine every year. Why can't she remember?

Rosa inhales. This one must be seven feet tall. It is a pleasant-looking tree with a symmetrical shape. Maud has a good eye for picking trees and now she is decorating it with her usual meticulous attention to detail. Each year Maud performs her Christmas-tree-decorating ritual. First, she puts the lights on. Next, she hangs the round white satin balls. Then she winds two strings of cranberries around and around.

Every December, two weeks before Christmas, Rosa sets a tin bowl filled with fresh cranberries on her lap and holds a needle with a double string of thread in her right hand — forcing one cranberry after another on the needle and along the thread. This is Rosa's part in the ritual: she puts the Peter, Paul and Mary holiday-concert cassette in the stereo, while Maud gets the box of decorations from their locker in the basement. Rosa makes the long chains of cranberries while Maud puts the lights on the tree and then hangs the white balls.

Rosa exhales, forcing grey smoke out through rounded lips. Once the chains of sour red berries are in place, Maud drapes the icicles — those delicate shimmering threads of silver that remind Rosa of Christmas trees from when she was growing up — over the branches. Then it is time to sit back and drink hot chocolate with whipped cream and admire their creation.

In the evenings over the next week they will wrap their gifts and place them beneath the tree. Maud, a lawyer by profession but an artist at heart, usually wraps Rosa's gifts when she has finished with her own. Maud takes pride in decorating the presents to look extraordinary, with green or red wool wrapped around the shiny silver foil paper and fashioned into slender bows on top. Sometimes she ties miniature candy canes into the bows. Last year she decorated the gifts with tiny foil-covered chocolate Santas.

Rosa, a social worker by profession and a social worker

at heart, finds December the most exhausting month of
the year. She comes home from work each evening feeling
tired and completely inadequate.

Her clients, mostly women and their children, are
despondent because they can't afford the traditional
Christmas feast, can't afford warm boots and snowsuits
and hats and mittens, can't afford the tree or toys to go
under it. The mothers worry about paying the rent and
the phone bill, worry about having enough money to buy
food as they struggle through the weeks of each long
month. They are perpetually nervous and weary from
worry.

Rosa patiently explains the latest budget cuts in social
services to each woman and refers her to one or two of the
over-burdened community groups that offer assistance at
Christmas. Sometimes she suggests a disheartened woman
contact the local advocacy group and join the fight against
poverty. Rosa urges them to educate themselves and to
rebel against their demeaning situation; at the same time,
she feels as pessimistic as the helpless women. They know
governments are made up of wealthy white male lawyers
and businessmen who never listen to the poor.

Rosa inhales and puts the cigarette in the ashtray.

Maud is singing along with Peter, Paul and Mary as she
works on the tree. "Once in a year it is not thought amiss,
to visit our neighbours and sing out like thissss." She is a
little off key but sings with feeling. "Of friendship and
love, good neighbours abound, and peace and goodwill
the whole year a-ro-undddd."

Maud adores the Christmas season and all the rituals.
Rosa thinks of her as being childlike in her devotion to
the holiday. Maud watches every Christmas show on

television, the made-for-TV movies, the cartoon shows, the Christmas episodes of all the regular shows, and the old Christmas movies like *It's a Wonderful Life* and *White Christmas.*

The only part of the ritual Maud dislikes is shopping for Christmas gifts. Rosa agrees wholeheartedly. Buying gifts is the most commercial aspect of Christmas and the most stressful. She wants her gifts to give pleasure, but it is not as easy as it sounds. And she always feels guilty when she spends money on expensive presents, on luxuries like black kid gloves for her mother and brightly-patterned silk scarves for Maud's sisters, knowing her clients are struggling just to feed themselves and their children.

Rosa stares at the bowl of cranberries and feels like crying. We demean our relationship by separating at Christmas, she says to Maud in her head. Do you think we would spend Christmas apart if we were a woman-man couple? Be honest with me. Rosa shoves the needle through a soft cranberry, keeping her head bent forward to hide the tears in her eyes. To say it like that might seem like she is criticizing Maud. Juice squishes onto her fingers, leaving a dark red stain. She sniffs quietly and clears away a tear with her thumb.

Rosa feels weak when she cries. Especially when Maud watches calmly, seeming to ignore the tears, the way she did a few weeks ago when Rosa was crying about a client.

On a day when she was feeling especially desperate, Janet Powers used her sister's credit card to buy winter coats for herself and her son, plus a set of pretty sheets and two down-filled pillows for her bed. She had never, she explained later to Rosa, bought sheets in her entire life. She always used hand-me-down sheets. She didn't mind hand-me-downs, it was just that for once she wanted brand-new sheets, and she wanted sheets that pleased her. She'd been having trouble sleeping at night and thought maybe soft pillows would help. Now her sister would have to make the monthly credit card payments to the bank and was furious and had told their whole family that Janet was a thief and was threatening to have her charged with stealing the credit card. What could Janet do? She didn't have the money to pay her sister back. She was so depressed she couldn't get out of bed some days. Her son sat on her lap, never uttering a sound. His silence and skinny hair and pinched face worried Rosa.

She couldn't stop thinking about Janet Powers and her small son. By the time Rosa opened the door of the apartment that evening, there were tears in her eyes. Within the safety of her home, the sobs started and she couldn't seem to stop.

Maud sat across from her and said, "You don't do them any good when you get so emotionally involved. Because that's not what they need. Where would I be if I got emotional about every client? And I could, believe you me. I'm already swamped with calls from women whose former spouses are demanding custody. These men ignore their kids all year but when Christmas rolls around suddenly they want them. Just because it's Christmas. You should get out of social work," Maud said sternly. "You should get out of direct service. You care too much."

Rosa picks up the cigarette and inhales. She hates crying. Maud never cries. Not once in their four years together has she known Maud to cry. What does Maud do with her pain and tears?

Rosa exhales and puts the cigarette out in the ashtray

with rapid stabbing motions. She understands that Maud wants to solve her problems for her and take away the pain, but she wishes Maud would say, instead, No wonder you're crying. You must feel awful for Janet Powers. Isn't life a bummer sometimes.

She wishes Maud would put her arms around her and say, Cry, let it all out.

But that is not Maud's way.

Rosa bends her head and forces herself to concentrate on her own problems. I love Maud. I want to spend Christmas with her. Is that asking so much?

So many of their friends do the same thing — they ignore their relationships, ignore their partners, to spend Christmas with their families. They act as if they are single women without any ties except to family — ties to their biological families, not to their family of lesbian friends. It's not fair.

Maybe it is the feeling of despair that makes Rosa speak the next words that enter her mind. "Why do we bother with a tree when we won't be here for Christmas?" She looks up, watching Maud and waiting for her response.

Maud does not seem to hear the anger. "We have to have a tree," she said calmly, as if it were a fact of life like November leading to December. "It's Christmas." She opens a small box and places a white ball in the palm of her hand. "Are those berries ready yet?"

"No." Rosa shoves the needle through a soft berry and slides the berry down the thread. She has started and she can't stop. "This is a fraud," she says, not looking at Maud. "Are we a couple or are we not? Your sisters and their husbands don't spend Christmas apart. They

wouldn't dream of separating at Christmas. Why do we?"
She didn't mean to say it like that. She looks up.

Maud is cradling the white ornament in her hand,
stroking the soft satin with a forefinger. "We've been
through this before. Do we have to go through it every
year? Why do you have to spoil everything!"

Rosa watches Maud hang the white ball from a branch,
then take another ball from the box and move to the other
side of the tree.

"I don't want to spoil everything, but I want to talk
about it. I don't understand why we have to spend Christmas apart."

Maud turns to look at her. "You know why we have to.
Talk! It never ends. We talk and talk but what does it do?
Everything's been arranged. Why are you making an issue
of this? Why are you doing this? Because Helen and her
new lover are spending Christmas together? Is that it?"

Rosa picks up a berry and pushes the needle into the
soft centre. "This has nothing to do with Helen and
Nawal. And don't raise your voice to me. If you don't want
to talk about it, say so, and tell me why you don't want to
talk about it. But don't yell."

There is silence in the room. Maud hangs white balls
on the tree. Rosa bends forward and works on the growing
chain of berries.

I tried, Rosa thinks. Maud doesn't want to deal with it.
So we will pretend. Always pretending that nothing is
wrong. There's no problem. We're lesbians, but let's not
make a big deal of it. No fuss, no muss, no disturbance.
Let's just pretend we are two women who live together
because it's convenient. It's cheaper this way, sharing ex-
penses. And we have each other for company. It's simply

companionship. Whatever we do, don't demand that we act like a couple or be treated like a couple. We are not married. We have no status, no recognition, no nothing. That's it. We're nothing. We're just two women who happen to live together. Good friends, that's all. Nothing more.

Rosa's hands move quickly, forcing one berry after another onto the needle and along the thread. Her throat aches. Why am I making this fuss? That's all we are. Why pretend? We are simply two women living together.

Her hands stop moving.

But we are more. We're much more. We love each other. We are a couple. Except at Christmas. The tears are back, threatening to spill down her cheeks.

She sets the bowl on the floor and goes into the bathroom. Closing the door behind her, she leans across the sink. Her face, reflected in the mirror, looks grim. Am I always this pale? She bends forward to study the colour of her skin. Maybe it does have something to do with Helen and Nawal spending Christmas together. I envy them, envy their excitement and their easy decision to spend Christmas with each other.

There is a knock at the door. "Are you okay?"

Rosa clears her throat and watches herself answer. "I'm alive and breathing."

That's nasty. I'm sorry Maud. You don't deserve it. The white face is motionless, staring back at her. There is silence in her head as she glares at the mirror.

"May I come in?" The door opens and Maud peeks around the edge. She pushes the door wide open and walks in. "What's up?"

Rosa turns from the mirror. "It's the pretending. We

pretend we're a couple. We pretend we're not a couple. It depends on the situation. We send a Christmas card to Helen and Nawal and sign both our names. I send one to my mother and sign only my name." She looks at Maud, looks into her eyes. "Why can't we spend Christmas together?"

Maud stares at Rosa for a moment before speaking.

"You think I don't care? I hate leaving you. But what do you want me to do about it? It's a hopeless situation. Why do you have to make it harder?"

Rosa says nothing. Each year she resents spending Christmas away from Maud, resents it more than she knows how to express, and this year she is determined to change it. But how? She swallows to stop the tears. She wants to say, It is connected to our lives as lesbians and that makes our separation feel worse — if that's possible. It's a betrayal of our lives. We are denying our love.

"Why are you so quiet? Come back to the living room." Maud rests a hand on Rosa's shoulder. "I'll help you string the rest of the cranberries."

Rosa tilts her head and brushes her cheek along Maud's hand. "I feel like I'm denying who I am. I love you and I want the whole world to know. I want everyone to see us as a couple. What's wrong with that?"

"There's nothing wrong with that. It's the most natural thing in this world. But you make yourself sick about it because you take all this too seriously, and it's not worth it. Come on. Wash your face."

Maud watches as Rosa turns on the cold water tap and splashes water on her face. She follows Rosa into the living room and sits on the floor in front of Rosa's chair, her shoulders between Rosa's knees.

"If you want to know what I think, I think straights get carried away with this togetherness business." Maud turns to look up at Rosa. "They have to do every single thing together. We don't have to imitate them. Why should we?"

Rosa shrugs and reaches for a cigarette and the orange lighter. "Are you saying we spend Christmas apart because we want to? Not because we're lesbians?" She lights the cigarette and inhales.

"No. You know I don't mean that. Spending Christmas together doesn't make us a couple and spending it apart doesn't stop us from being a couple. It's how we feel about each other that matters."

Rosa exhales forcefully. "Yeah. But there's something wrong with that logic. But it doesn't matter. Maud, I want to be with you at Christmas. That's all I want."

"Yes and you want to see your mother too. I want to see my family. They live six hundred miles apart. What do you think we can do? It's an impossible situation."

"It's not six hundred miles from Kingston to Kitchener."

"It might as well be. It's too far to spend Christmas together and with both our families because we'd spend all day on the 401. We'd be tired and we wouldn't see anyone. That's no way to spend Christmas."

Rosa reaches out to stroke Maud's hair. "I know."

Maud sighs loudly. "You always want too much. You know that, don't you. You want too much."

"Is it too much to want to spend Christmas with you!"

"Look who's raising her voice now."

Rosa sighs, a small sigh. She bends forward and kisses the top of Maud's head. "The tree is nice, huh."

Maud turns and takes Rosa's hand. "Yeah. Best tree we've ever had. You know there's no way we can do it because we can't be together and be with our families. There's no way. Why can't you accept it?"

Rosa nods.

"But I've got an idea." Maud squeezes Rosa's hand and smiles. "We could have our own Christmas together, before we leave. Our own Christmas with a meal and we'd open presents. The whole works. What do you think? I like it."

"It wouldn't be the same."

"Damn, Rosa, you drive me cuckoo. Stubborn! You invented the word."

"I want to spend Christmas with you."

"Yes, well, do you have any ideas?"

Rosa shrugs, thinking, What are our options?

"When you figure it out, let me know. I'm out of ideas." Maud stands up and walks toward the tree.

Rosa picks up the bowl and sits it on her lap. Maud is right. We don't have to mimic het couples. She squashes a soft berry when she tries to force it on the needle. I want to be with Maud. Red juice darkens her stained fingers. I want to be with my mother too. And Maud wants to be with her parents and sisters.

She looks at Maud. Before we leave we could have a Christmas dinner here with our friends, our family of women. A lesbian Christmas. No, a lesbian solstice. Yes, that's it. We could invite Helen and Nawal, and Liam, Maryse and Linda. It won't be the same as spending Christmas with Maud, but . . . the fist in her stomach relaxes a little. And Ingrid and Eileen, and Giselle. A lesbian winter solstice celebration.

"What kind of celebration would we have here?"

Maud is winding the first chain of cranberries around the tree. She pauses and turns to look at Rosa. "It could just be the two of us or we could invite some friends for a Christmas meal. We could all sit around the tree and sing carols. What do you think? How about the Sunday before Christmas? Next Sunday. We'll invite Helen and Nawal. And your friend Liam."

Rosa is amazed, and it is not the first time this has happened, that Maud is thinking the very same thing that she is thinking. "Okay, let's do that. And how about we invite Giselle and Maryse and Linda and Ingrid and Eileen?" Rosa pushes the needle through a hard berry, and then another hard one. The berries slide easily along the wet thread.

"No, not Eileen and Ingrid. I don't want Eileen here."

"Why not?"

"I don't like Eileen. Don't ask me why because I don't know. I just don't like her."

"I didn't know that you didn't like her."

"Do you like her? How can you like her. She's always saying hurtful things to Ingrid. She's got a mean streak in her that pisses me off."

"I know. It bothers me sometimes. But, Maud, I really like Ingrid. We've been friends for years and I want her to be here with us."

"Okay then, invite them if you want to."

"Are you sure?"

"Yes, invite them. But I'm warning you I might say something to Eileen, because if she starts on at Ingrid I won't be able to stop myself."

"Okay," Rosa agrees, hoping Eileen will be on her best

behaviour. She is so encouraged by the change in mood that she decides to tell Maud some of the other ideas she has about Christmas. "Maud, let's make it a different kind of holiday celebration. Like, let's not have turkey. Let's have a vegetarian meal instead. And we won't wrap the presents in paper. We'll use tea towels or cloth napkins to spare some trees. Let's go through the cookbooks when we're done. We'll make something special. How does that sound?" Rosa laughs. "How about we ask everyone to bring a dish. A lesbian pot-luck winter solstice dinner." The words roll off her tongue.

"That's it," says Maud. "We'll start a new tradition. I'll make the pudding. I've always wanted to try making a Christmas pudding. Do you think Helen would make some bread? There's nothing like her bread."

"Yeah." Rosa remembers the taste of Helen's bread as she quietly hums along with her favourite carol. She feels excited at the thought of having all their friends together for a solstice dinner. Next year, she decides to herself, we will do it differently. Next year, I will insist that we spend Christmas Day together. Somehow we'll find a way to do it. I have a year to think of a way around it. Maybe we won't see our families. Maybe we'll stay here, just the two of us. Rosa sighs. But I've always spent Christmas with Mom.

She slides a cranberry easily along the needle, then another one and another, and sings softly with Peter, Paul and Mary. "O sing our songs and raise the Torah, raise the Torah, right the wrongs and light menorah, light menorah."

Maud is standing back, admiring the tree.

"Why must it be a Scots pine? I can never remember."

"It's the perfect Christmas tree because it's bushy and beautiful. Most people get a spruce. Even those artificial trees are made to look like spruces. But a Scots pine is better." Maud turns to look at Rosa. "Is the next chain ready yet?"

Rosa shakes her head. "It's getting there." She uses both hands to lift the gigantic necklace of cranberries from the tin bowl for Maud to see. "Why don't you sit beside me while I finish it."

"This is the last ball," Maud warns. She hangs it on a low branch and then sits beside Rosa. "I love you, Rosa."

"Yeah, I know." Rosa squeezes her hand, leaving a faint blush of squashed cranberry juice on Maud's thumb.

Delila and Ms. MacLeod

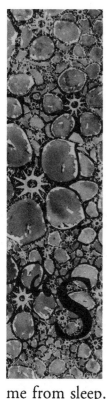

top that! STOP THAT!"

His voice shoots through the silence with frightening clarity, through the floor between his apartment and mine, tearing me from sleep.

"Do that one more time and I'll kill you!"

Jessica crawls into bed with me. "I want a duvet just like this one for my bed, for Christmas. Are you awake? One that has a beige cover, like yours."

I sigh and open my eyes. The Saturday sun is shining, filling my bedroom with light. I had planned to sleep in today, to wake gently when my body decided it was time.

"Why does Michael scream at his kids so much?"

"I don't know, Ms. MacLeod." I call her Ms. MacLeod because it makes her feel eighteen instead of thirteen. I keep meaning to warn her that eighteen isn't all it's cracked up to be, and that thirty-three is much better. "He is, perhaps, a frustrated man."

"Yeah. But why doesn't he do something about it? 'Steada taking it out on his kids."

"It isn't that simple." Or is it? I am not up to these philosophical discussions first thing in the morning.

The inevitable wail from a child rises up to us from the apartment below, followed by, *"Shut up! Stop that! Stop crying!"* It occurs to me, for the nth time, that I have a responsibility to respond seriously to my daughter's questions.

"Michael's a tense kind of person. He's not well-suited to having kids. Remember the time he tried to fix our hall light? Such a simple job. He cursed and muttered the whole time, and didn't fix it in the end. He may not be doing what he really wants to do with his life. What do you think?"

"He's a turd!"

"Jessica!"

She laughs, with no hint of apology, as she looks over at me. "What are you doing today?"

"Nothing special. I'm going into work this afternoon."

"Awwww Mum!"

"I must, Jess. We need the money. You need a pair of jeans and new boots. I want a perm. This overtime money makes the difference. It'll just be for a couple of hours. What are your plans? Aren't you going somewhere with Freddie?"

"Yeah. Freddie and I are going to the library and her Mum's taking us to her granny's farm this afternoon."

"Sounds like fun. Shall we have pancakes for breakfast, Ms. MacLeod?"

"Yeah!"

Delila and Ms. MacLeod

I roll over and reluctantly leave my bed. In the bathroom I stretch and yawn and pee. In the kitchen the first thing I do is plug in the kettle. This is my favourite room. When we first moved in, Jess and I painted the walls off-white and the cupboards pale yellow. There are two windows, one facing south and the other facing east, and the room fills with sun on bright days.

After breakfast we dress and Jess goes off to meet Freddie at the library. I linger over a third cup of coffee, savouring the peace and solitude, before turning my attention to twenty-four hours of dirty dishes.

I am patiently scrubbing at some cheese sauce which is glued to the rim of a plate, and wondering at the same time if I should dump the dirty dishwater, when the phone rings. I let the plate slide back into the water and grab the tea towel from the counter, drying my hands as I walk toward the phone. I lift the receiver during the second ring.

"Hello."

"Hello! How are you today?"

There is a long silence while I consider the question and the caller. I do not recognize the voice. He speaks with the intimacy of a lover. Or a salesman.

"I'm fine," I venture, cautiously.

"And how would you like an erotic phone call this morning?"

I answer quickly, "No, thank you. I don't have time." And I hang up.

I return to the dirty dishwater and attack the dried cheese with renewed energy. What if he phones right back? I won't answer the phone. Will that call be the beginning of a string of similar calls?

I thanked him. Imagine that. What a dummy. No, what a well-brought-up woman I am, that I thank an obscene caller. The blob of cheese gives way and drops into the water. I rinse the soap from the plate and prop the plate in the rack. As I fill the basin with clean water, I wonder what he would have said if Jess had answered the phone. Everyone told me bringing up a child alone wouldn't be easy. But some days it seems like there's one thing after another to worry about. How can I protect her from an obscene phone call?

I leave the apartment at noon, after vacuuming the whole place and washing the kitchen floor. While I stand at the bus stop, a carload of boys drives past. They honk and yell at me and wave and honk some more in simulated friendliness. I pretend they do not exist. There must be a better way to handle such situations, but I don't know what it is.

At work I manipulate the keyboard to produce the required documents, not paying much attention to what I am doing. The obscene phone call haunts me. I feel vulnerable. He could be someone who knows me; he may have picked my number from the phone book; or, he may have dialled randomly. What if he knows my address? That is frightening. That's something to worry about. He could extend his violence to a physical assault. Jess and I should take a self-defence course.

All the way home on the bus I think about Jess. I hate leaving her alone, especially for hours at a time. Usually I am proud of her independence, but the obscene caller has reminded me that she lacks experience in coping with many aspects of life.

When I open the apartment door at 7 pm, I find

myself praying to some unknown being that Jess will be
there, sheltered and safe from all harshness and harm.

She is stretched out on the chesterfield, eyes closed,
looking tired and pale. Freddie is curled up in a chair,
watching TV.

"Hi there, Delila," Freddie says to me.

Freddie calls everyone Delila. I found this disconcert-
ing at first and questioned Jess about it.

"Freddie calls everyone Delila," Jess assured me. "It's
just one of her idiosyncrasies."

"Idiosyncrasies?"

"Yeah, you know, something that's just her."

"I know what idiosyncrasies means," I said indignantly.
"I'm merely surprised that you do."

"Hi, Delila." When Freddie calls me Delila I call her
Delila back. "Are you okay, Jess?"

"O Mum, am I glad to see you. It started. My period. I
think. My stomach hurts." She sounds like a battered
child, not the blossoming woman I usually live with.

I feel threads of panic spinning through my body. I am
in charge here, I tell myself firmly, sternly. "Jessie, how
wonderful. When did all this happen?"

"A while ago. When we got home there was blood on
my pants, so I changed them. And now my stomach
hurts."

I find myself speaking rapidly. "I'll get you one of my
pills, for cramps. You certainly won't have to suffer with
cramps the way I did for years. I'll phone Ellen on Monday and make an appointment. I wonder if you're too
young to take this drug. We'll see what Ellen says. We'll
ask her, at the same time, if she thinks you're too young
for sponges. Would you like to use sponges instead of

tampons? They don't recommend tampons for women under 18, but I don't know about sponges. What harm could they do? Use pads until we see Ellen. I'll go to the store and get some." I sit on the chesterfield and hug her. "I'll make us hot chocolate when I get back from the store. Everything will be alright. Are you okay?"

"Yeah."

As I hurry down the hall I hear Freddie say, "Sponges? What's that?"

Jess chuckles.

I make a quick dash around the apartment, taking *Our Bodies Our Selves* from the bookcase in the kitchen, and return to the living room. Freddie is sitting beside Jess on the sofa. She watches from a solemn face as I hand Jess the tablet and a glass of milk. I lay the book between them. "Read up on menstruation while I'm gone."

When I return from the store, they are huddled together with the open book. I put Jess into a hot bath. She's been bathing alone for many years now but, much to my surprise, she seems to enjoy having me fill the tub for her and sit on the toilet to chat and then wrap her in a towel when she steps out. I show her how to use the pad.

I make hot chocolate for the three of us and we settle on the chesterfield. "Are you staying the night, Delila?"

Freddie nods and giggles.

"Anything else happen today, Ms. MacLeod?"

Jess is returning to her former self. "Mr. Magalhaes was fighting with Jean-Paul's father on the street outside our building."

Mr. Magalhaes lives in the apartment building to the left of ours. He owns it and lives with his family in the basement apartment and rents out the other apartments.

Jean-Paul and his father live in the third-floor apartment in the building to the right.

"What was it about?"

"O, I don't know. Something about the garage Mr. Magalhaes is building in his backyard, making noise all the time, and not having a building permit. The police came. There were three cruisers."

"Sounds unpleasant." I worry about this neighbour-hood and its influence on Jess. On both of us, for that matter. Teenage boys wander the streets at night, looking for entertainment. Last month three of them raped a woman behind the Seven-Eleven. And then there's Michael downstairs, the teacher who hates children — especially his own. But housing is hard to find and I can't afford the nicer areas. I wish we could live somewhere that had lots of grass and tall trees and quiet neighbours.

"Naw," says Freddie. "It was exciting. What an exciting day."

"O yeah," Jess agrees. "Three cruisers and everybody was yelling and everything."

"Did you get some library books?"

"Yeah, I got two, and then we drove to the farm and we helped Freddie's granny make an apple pie and we ate it before supper. She let us eat the whole thing ourselves. And we drank well water and she let us feed the chickens and we had meat pie for supper."

"Jess, do you have any questions about menstruation?"

"Not now. Maybe later."

"Delila?"

"Naw. I know all about it. I got mine last year."

I still have to tell Jess about the obscene phone call, to warn her. Tomorrow. Enough has happened today.

I take the beige duvet from my bed and spread it over us. Jess sits in the middle, between Freddie and I, and we watch an old movie on TV. It's a black and white TV. Jess moans every so often that Everyone has a colour TV. I wish I could give her a colour TV. I get so tired of saying we can't afford it. And she must get tired of hearing me say it.

After the movie ends, with the immaculate socialite marrying the dedicated doctor, we prepare for bed. Jess takes a second tablet and changes the pad. Freddie watches with keen interest. Before turning out the bedroom light, I give Jess and Freddie a hug and say, "Pleasant dreams. I'm sleeping in tomorrow so try to be quiet when you get up, would you."

I am dreaming about living in a drafty mansion with ten kids and three dogs. It is a busy dream. Just as we are sitting down to a meal of dandelions, grass and poplar leaves, I hear a police siren. The siren changes to a ringing phone and I am awake.

Jess answers the phone, speaking quiet and indistinct phrases. I leave the warm bed, reluctantly, and stumble into the kitchen. The room looks drab. I can see a cloudy sky through the window, beyond Jess' head.

"Good morning, Mum. It's Granddad. She's up now, Granddad. Here she is."

Dad wants to remind me of the dinner tonight, in honour of their thirty-fifth wedding anniversary. And to let me know that Sears is having a sale. Don't I want a washing machine? Yes, I tell him, I want an apartment-size washer and a perm and winter boots for Jess and a colour TV, and most of all I want a telephone answering machine, but Sears doesn't accept buttons and I don't have money.

He is not amused. "We'll expect you at five," he orders,

before hanging up.

I sit down, immediately regretting my anger. I pick up the receiver and dial. He answers during the first ring.

"Hello, Dad. I'm sorry about my smart mouth. Yesterday was a rough day."

"Never you mind, love. Have a strong cup of coffee. Come over early and I'll take Jessie to the flea market."

I check on Jess and Freddie — they are watching *Star Trek* — and head back to bed. Just as I am drifting off, his voice roars loud and clear, as if he is beside me rather than in the apartment below. *"JON-A-THAN! Look what he's done. Damn him! Jonathan! Where is he! Jonathan, get in here. Right now!"*

Why does he scream at his kids so much? How dare he inflict his anger on us. I should wear my boots and stomp around, banging the rigid leather soles on the hardwood floors. See how he feels when loud noise disturbs his life. I wait for the crying and a minute later it starts. Turning over, with one quick movement I pull the duvet around my head.

I wake a second time to the ringing phone. Jess answers it, but this time her muttering quickly becomes audible. "What? What did you say?"

I throw myself out of bed and down the hall, into the dark kitchen. Jess looks stunned. I grab the phone from her.

"Hello."

"How are you this morning?"

"You. You're a sick excuse for a person, aren't you. Assaulting a child! GET HELP! See a doctor. Don't phone here again. Never. Or I'll track you down and squeeze the life out of your puny balls. In a garlic press! Do you understand? I've got a garlic press right here waiting for you. You're sick, Sick, SICK!"

I hang up and sit down, trembling. Jess stands in the same spot, staring at me. Freddie, in the doorway, looks from Jess to me and back to Jess.

"What did he say?" I feel I am going about this the wrong way. But what would be a better way? Jess looks at Freddie, then back to me. "I'm not angry at you, Jess. I'm furious at him. What did he say?"

"Cut that out! STOP THAT! Jonathan!"

I moan and bury my face in my hands. Jess pats my shoulder. "It's alright, Mum. I'll make you some coffee."

I hear Freddie seat herself at the table. Damn him to eternal torment. How could he do that to a child? I uncover my face. Jess is scooping ground coffee and dumping it into the filter. Freddie is watching me. It could be worse. Much worse.

"He said," Jess is facing the window and the overcast sky, "that he wanted to suck my breasts." She turns to face me.

Where has this child acquired such strength?

"He phoned yesterday, after you left to meet Freddie at the library. I was going to warn you, today, about him." The child downstairs starts bawling, loudly and with gusto. "Let's have some coffee and I'll tell you about it. We'll have to be prepared, in case he dares to phone again." I walk across the room and put my arms around Jess.

"Shut up! Do you hear me? Stop that. STOP CRYING!"

Freddie clears her throat. "My mother's had enough of the city. She says we're moving to my granny's farm after Christmas."

"Do you have room for two more?"

Freddie giggles. "I'll ask her."

"Don't be silly, Mum." Jess gives me a stern frown. "We're alright here."

"Yes. I suppose we are. Well, what are you two making for breakfast?"

Freddie makes toast, Jess makes scrambled eggs, and I drink coffee and talk. "I'll buy a whistle and leave it beside the phone. If he phones again, we'll blow the whistle into the receiver and rupture his eardrum." I don't like the satisfaction I feel when I say 'rupture his eardrum.'

Freddie leans on the counter, watching Jess pour orange juice into glasses. She grins at Jess and says, "What do you think, Delila?"

A Guilty Move

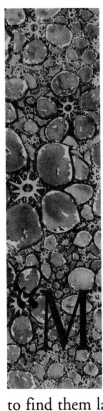

M UM!"

I stand absolutely still, looking at the screws and bolts in my hand and wondering what to do with them so I will be able to find them later. Will she call a second time? I'll never get the kitchen table back together if I lose these screws and bolts. I am tempted to duck into the hall closet and hide, tempted also to giggle, but more than anything I want to yell, LEAVE ME ALONE!

"Maaaum!"

I stuff the bolts and screws in the pocket of my jeans. Will she call a third time? What does she want? I am a heartless mother to ignore the calls of my daughter. How can I not respond to my beloved child.

"Mum? Where are you? Maaaum!"

Sometimes when I am shopping alone (and what bliss

it is, to shop alone) I hear a voice call *Mom* and I turn automatically. I am conditioned to respond to that one word. It is as familiar to me as my given name.

Sometimes I make myself stay where I am when Jess calls me, although it takes immense willpower to stop myself from running to her. Other times, times like today when I am frustrated within myself, I resent her demands. It is easier to stay where I am on the days when I feel resentful.

"What do you want, Jessica? I'm busy." I speak slowly and distinctly, using her full name so she will know I am not pleased.

We are moving today. I am frantic. The two are definitely related.

When I got the promotion at work last month, the first thing I did was start looking for another place to live. This promotion is making a big difference in our lives. I have wanted to move for a long time — in fact, it's been my goal for years to get out of this concrete neighbourhood and into a nice area with grass and trees and fresh air.

I asked my friend Peig if she would drive me around to see some places for rent. When I told her I wanted to move to a nice neighbourhood, she wanted to know what I meant by *nice*.

Peig's question annoyed me. She knows what nice means. She has lived in nice neighbourhoods all her life. She grew up with a silver-plated spoon in her mouth and parents who paid for violin lessons and ski lessons and braces to straighten her teeth, plus six years of university. These days she makes enough money to live almost anywhere in the city, thanks to two university degrees and her

Daddy's connections in the business community, but she chooses to live in a trendy working-class area. She owns the red-brick house she lives in and the oak tree in the front yard, or at least she has a mortgage. Her Daddy gave her the down payment for the house. And Peig drives a nice car, one of those sporty imports. I wish I could afford a car.

I grew up with a stainless-steel spoon in my mouth, in a poor neighbourhood. I want out. I want to live on a street of nice houses, with lush green lawns and a feeling of space and peacefulness. Thirty-four years of poverty is enough for me.

I feel guilty about it, though, that I want to be up-wardly mobile. I feel like I'm not politically correct. Like I'm letting the whole feminist movement down. But I want choices in my life. Is that asking for so much?

My next goal is to buy a car. Then, one day, I'd like to buy a house. Nothing spectacular. A small bungalow covered in maintenance-free vinyl siding would suit me. It will be in a nice neighbourhood, of course.

Jess appears beside me, frowning. She hasn't smiled at me for days although it feels like weeks. Maybe it has been weeks. I have become the enemy. I am bringing turmoil into her life and uprooting her.

She looks down at her bare feet and wiggles her toes. "Have you seen my running shoes? I can't find them any-where."

Her toe-nails are painted black, to match her finger-nails. I tell myself this is just a stage she is going through. This will pass. And I try to be grateful it's merely black nail polish and not drugs or booze or cigarettes or sex, especially unprotected sex. Jess brings home some hair-raising stories about kids at school: a classmate is in the psychiatric hospital after overdosing on her mother's prescription drugs; her best friend's sister is pregnant and trying to decide whether to have an abortion or go through with the pregnancy and if she continues with the pregnancy will she give the baby up for adoption or finish high school while bringing the child up and she's only in grade ten; and then there's the sixteen-year-old girl down the street who is facing drunk-driving charges.

"I left my runners in the kitchen last night." Her voice has an accusing tone lately. "All my other shoes are packed."

"You shouldn't have left them lying around. I must have packed them this morning. Look in the box in the kitchen, beside the fridge, the one marked 'sheets and towels.' I think I threw some runners in there."

She shakes her head, as if her mother is quite impossible. Her silent rebukes can hurt more than the words she flings at me when she is angry. She knows me well and knows exactly how to hurt me. Last night, as I was trying to get the last-minute packing done, she told me I am a bad mother for taking her away from her friends.

"There's nothing wrong with this neighbourhood," she said. "I like it here. We're close to everything and I can walk where I want. All my friends are here. You're just a snob!"

This is how a fourteen year old drives her thirty-four-year-old mother to the brink of despair. No one wants to be called a snob. And certainly no one wants to be called a bad mother.

Anyway, Peig drove me around for a few evenings last month until I found a place to rent. Today we are moving out of this cramped downtown apartment to a west-end suburb with two birch trees on the front lawn. Jess is not pleased. I'm doing this for her, but she doesn't appreciate it. She doesn't want to leave this familiar neighbourhood and her friends.

I can't wait to get away. No more motorcycles roaring up and down the street, going through thirteen gears in one block. No more teenaged boys harassing me as I walk to the bus stop. No more dragging our bicycles up and down three flights of stairs, because you can be sure they would be gone in an hour if we left them chained to the railing at the front door of the building. And no more listening to the man downstairs yell at his wife and scream at their kids.

I bend down to pick up the screwdriver and stay there, crouched down, looking around the room. What else has to be done? All our belongings are packed in boxes or laying in pieces on the floor. The beds are apart. The kitchen table is in pieces, and the screws and bolts are in my pocket. The sofa is intact. Will it survive the move? It's old. It was already old when I bought it from the second-hand store six years ago.

Jess was eight then. She leaned against the arm, strok-ing the matching pillow with her right hand, and told the salesperson that we were going to buy a rug next — when I had enough money saved up. Her truthfulness about money made me uncomfortable. We got the rug the fol-lowing year, and now it's rolled up and tied with twine beside the sofa.

The door bell rings. It's the woman from downstairs, holding a box of muffins and smiling shyly. "I'm sorry you're leaving," she says, holding out the box.

I take the muffins. Don't cry. Swallow once. Twice. A third time.

I've never told her it drives me crazy, listening to her husband yell at her and their two sons. It must make her crazy too. Why does she stay? I've never dared ask her. We have a casual relationship, hello and a few words about the weather when we meet in the hall.

I hear voices and footsteps on the stairs and then familiar faces appear: Jocelyne and Freida, Ann holding baby Lancy, Linn, Peig, and Susannah.

My neighbour turns and walks downstairs, through the crowd of my friends. Her husband is one of the reasons I have to move. His loud angry voice, penetrating upward into my home, into my life, makes me anxious, makes me feel violent toward him.

I smile at my friends. "You're all here at the same time."

"You said eight-thirty and it's eight-thirty." Linn moves forward, leading the others past me into the apartment. She is my best friend, a darling woman with curly brown and grey hair and huge outrageous earrings. She comes around behind me and puts a hand on my shoulder. "How are you? Ready to move?"

"Frantic is the key word." I put the box of muffins on the floor.

"Don't worry. Don't get your britches in knots. We'll have you moved in no time." Linn hugs me. Her huge metal earring feels cold against my cheek. "Where's Jess?"

Jess appears as if on cue, wearing running shoes and grinning. "Hi!" She turns to Freida and Jocelyne, who have been together forever. They've even started looking alike, both with spiked black hair. "Where's the truck?"

Freida looks at Jocelyne, then at me, then Jess. "Hey!
That's what I forgot." Her eyes are large. "I knew I forgot
something. When I got up this morning I told Jocelyne
there was something I had to do today but I couldn't
remember what." She looks at Jocelyne. "I forgot the
truck."

Jocelyne mouths the words, Oh no.

I knew something would go wrong. We have to be out
by noon. All these women, ready to help me move, and no
truck. What will I do? How could Freida forget! I was
counting on her. Haven't I learned yet that you can't count
on anyone except yourself? Would the rental people keep
the truck for me, or would someone else have it by now?
I feel my body trembling inside, even though I stand
motionless beside Linn.

Jess laughs. "You can't fool me. Come on. Where is it?
Did you pull it up to the back door?"

Freida smiles. "You're too smart for me."

I am tempted to giggle, but more than anything I want
to cry. Inappropriate behaviour for an adult. I take a deep
breath and stuff my sweaty hands in the pockets of my
jeans. One hand grasps the collection of bolts and screws
that usually hold the kitchen table together. The other
hand holds two brass-coloured keys, the keys to our new
home.

Linn comes to my rescue. "Drive over to McDonald's.
Take my car. Get us some coffee and buns. We'll start
loading the truck." She hands me a ring of keys.

"I hate McDonald's." I know I sound just like Jess
when she is in one of her uncooperative moods, but I can't
help myself.

"Yes, yes, I know you do. It's against your principles.

But swallow them this morning. It's fast, it's cheap and it's convenient. Go. And remember to drive carefully." Linn turns to Jess. "You look after the baby, Jess. Okay?" She smiles at Lancy, who is squirming in Ann's arms. "So Ann can help with the move."

"Yeah, sure." Jess holds her arms open for Lancy.

"Where shall we start?" Peig looks around the room.

"Boxes first." Linn starts walking toward the kitchen. "Get all the boxes outside and load them in the truck. Is anyone good at packing a truck?"

"Hi! Having a party?" Suyuan stands in the open doorway, a package of paper cups tucked under one arm, a jug of orange juice dangling from each hand.

Jess laughs and shifts Lancy to her other hip. My daughter is smiling and laughing! "Hi, Suyuan. Are you good at packing a truck?"

Suyuan grins. "It's one of my best party tricks."

Everyone laughs, even me.

Linn takes the jugs of juice from Suyuan. "I'll put these in the fridge. Let's get going here, women."

Peig smiles at me with her nice straight teeth and comes over to where I'm standing. "Go on," she says quietly. "Don't worry. Everything is under control. Linn's in charge and Suyuan will pack the truck."

I bend my head and take a deep breath. Then I squeeze Peig's hand. I am blessed, to have these caring friends. What have I done to deserve such caring women in my life?

I am gone for much longer than I had expected. McDonald's is packed with people. The noisy and energetic children outnumber the adults. As usual, I choose the wrong line. I always do. Lines in banks, lines in grocery stores, I always head for the shortest one and it turns out to be the slowest one. After standing impatiently for ten minutes, but it feels like three hours, and just as I am getting close to the counter, the man ahead of me places an order that is surely intended to feed a small army. The young woman races around, piling styrofoam containers of food on the counter. Do they have to use styrofoam?

My impatience grows. I'm moving today and I don't have time to stand around doing nothing. I tell myself to relax, to take it easy since there is nothing else I can do.

As the young woman scurries back and forth, making the piles of styrofoam food higher and higher, a man walks over to her cash register. He looks cool and crisp in his white shirt and blue tie. He looks at the cash register, touches it once and smiles at the customer. "That'll be thirty-two eighty-five, sir."

I feel my anger, ever close, rising up. She does the hard work and he gets to take the money. Why doesn't he help her fill the order. Better still, why doesn't he fill the order while she takes the money?

I smile at her when it's my turn at the counter. A friendly smile. She's young, only a couple of years older than Jess.

When I get back to the apartment, everyone is working. Ann is downstairs handing my floor lamp to Suyuan in the nearly-full truck. Peig and Linn and Susannah are carrying my apartment-sized washer down the backstairs and telling each other how to do it. Freida is following them down the stairs with armfuls of clothes that she's taking to Peig's car.

My friends are doing all the work. I walk around the

vacant apartment, amazed at what they have accomplished. Jocelyne is whistling while scrubbing the bathtub. I find Jess in her empty bedroom, sitting on the floor with Lancy.

"I'm back."

They both look up. Lancy giggles and stretches out her arms. She likes, more than anything, to be held. At that age Jess wanted to be free to wander as she pleased.

"Hi, Mum. You were gone a long time."

Before I can answer, Linn appears at my side. "We're almost finished." She takes the bags of coffee and danish buns from me and yells, "There's coffee and food here! Anyone want a break?"

Jess picks up Lancy. The baby's chubby arms encircle my daughter's slender neck. My baby looks like a young mother.

Women start arriving in the bedroom. The first thing Ann does is take her baby from Jess. Lancy laughs and hugs Ann. Jess looks sad.

Freida holds the box of muffins. "I found these near the front door. Do you want them?"

"Yes. I forgot about them. They're from the woman downstairs." I take the box and put it beside the bags from McDonald's. "Thanks for getting it."

Linn hands out cups of coffee and cups of orange juice. Suyuan opens the box, takes a muffin, and passes the box around the room. Soon everyone is sitting on the floor, leaning against the bare walls, eating and drinking and talking. Ann feeds Lancy from a bottle of apple juice.

Jess sits close to me, eating a bun and drinking milk from a small carton. It is unusual for her to stay near me.

"Mum?"

"Yes." I reach over and run my fingers through her hair. She doesn't pull away.

"It looks funny in here without furniture."

I look around. This is not our home any more. It is a group of rooms with naked floors and walls, waiting for someone to move in and impose her personality on the space.

"It looks like it did when we moved in. You were little then. You wouldn't remember."

Jocelyne, leaning against Freida, asks, "What's your new home like?"

"It's great. The best part is there isn't anyone above us or beneath us. But wait until you see it. It's well-cared for and has hardwood floors that have been sanded and varnished or whatever it is they do to floors to make them shiny."

"Urethane?"

"Yes, that's it. It's a half-double. The kitchen is small. Every room has a window, even the bathroom. Jess and I like windows. There's a screened porch off the kitchen. The backyard is long and narrow and it's completely shaded by tall trees on three sides. There isn't much grass, because of the shade I guess. Upstairs we have three bedrooms. One for me and one for Jess and one for the TV."

"And it's in a *nice* neighbourhood?"

I look over at Peig and smile. "Yes, Peig, it's in a very nice neighbourhood."

Linn calls across the room. "Are you going to the dance tonight?"

"If I survive the move."

Linn shakes her head as she laughs and her metal earrings dance. "You always have to have a crisis. Don't sweat it. We're almost finished here and unloading at the new place will be fast. We'll be done in an hour or so and you'll be moved in in no time."

I look at Jess. She's grinning at me. At me! And her left eyebrow is raised, the way it does when she is genuinely amused. She says it makes her feel good to see me, the one who bosses her around, being bossed by Linn. I wink at her.

Freida stands up. "Let's finish up here."

My friends stand one by one, looking refreshed, and leave the room. Jocelyne starts gathering up the remnants of our feast, putting empty paper cups and containers back into the McDonald's bags. She has tendonitis in her shoulders, from playing softball, and can't lift furniture or boxes. Ann remains on the floor, rocking the sleeping baby in her arms.

"Well," I say to Jess, "shall we check all the cupboards and closets to make sure we haven't forgotten anything?"

"Yeah."

I watch her black fingertips drop the empty milk carton into a bag. What will I do if she paints her face with make-up and flutters her eyelashes at pimply boys? What will I do if she wants to drink beer and cuddle with one of the pimply boys? Will she like our new home? Will she make friends? Of course she will. She will adjust. This is a change for the better and we will both adjust. Change is good. Change is stimulating.

She turns to me. "Will you go to the dance tonight and leave me alone in the new house?"

"Would you mind?"

She shrugs.

"Let's see how we feel, later."

She shrugs again.

A Guilty Move

I need to go dancing. I need to feel part of the larger community, to be surrounded by dykes, and to escape the chaos and upheaval of this move. But Jess needs company and reassurance to help her adjust to these changes, changes she never wanted. It's always this way — balancing her needs and my needs and deciding which ones shall prevail. I'm working longer hours lately because of the promotion. She handles it well, for the most part. It's something else for me to feel guilty about. I must talk to her about all this, my guilt and our different needs.

We walk through the apartment, checking every closet and cupboard. In my room, what used to be my room, Jess makes a joke. She opens the closet door and says, "Your closet is empty. You must be right out of the closet, huh!"

She laughs and laughs, bent over, holding her belly. I chuckle. Her attempt at humour deserves some recognition.

It seems only minutes later that Linn walks into the room and finds us sitting in my empty closet, giggling.

"What are you pair doing in there? We're ready to leave," she announces.

"We're telling jokes. What starts with a 'G' like grape," Jess asks Linn, "and leaves purple stains on your soul?"

Linn stands, looking into the dark closet, smiling at us. "I don't know. What?"

Jess starts giggling again. "Gay guilt!" She yells triumphantly. "That's Mum's joke!"

Linn shakes her head. What does it mean, that the people I love keep shaking their heads at me?

"I hope you haven't inherited your mother's sense of humour."

Jess raises her left eyebrow. "Maybe yes. Maybe no." She winks at me.

Linn shakes her head again. "Come on, kids. Let's split this scene."

I'm ready to leave and excited about seeing our new home. And, now that it's happening, Jess seems fine. I don't have to feel guilty. Jess is right, though. I need to move for myself as much as for her.

"I'll lock up and leave the keys with the woman downstairs and meet you in the car." I smile at Jess and Linn, a smile of pure joy.

Beginnings

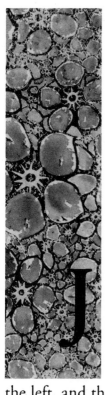

J enny stood on the front step, fumbling with the lock on the outside door and trembling slightly in the chilly January air. After turning the key to the right and to the left, and then to the right and to the left again, she took it out and peered at it in the darkness. She tried to ignore her feeling of panic. It must fit. This is the right key and the right door. She reinserted the key in the lock. It must. She withdrew the key a fraction of an inch and tried again, turning it to the right and then to the left.

She smiled when she felt the lock give and heard a distinct click. She shoved and the door opened with ease. She removed the key from the lock.

Stepping quickly inside, she closed the heavy door behind her and moved cautiously along the dimly-lit hall. Like an intruder, she held her breath as she walked past closed doors. She climbed the dark stairs with one hand on the railing to guide her and stopped at the door on the first landing. Bending down, she inserted another key into this lock. One half turn to the right and the door opened.

Jenny reached in and switched on the overhead light before entering the room. She closed the door and paused with her hand resting on the doorknob. Excitement danced through her as she surveyed the room, making her want to giggle. This was hers, her new home and the beginning of her new life.

It was a typical bed-sitting room. Each piece of furniture had an assigned spot in the small oblong space: bed, arborite table with two wooden chairs, bureau, easy chair, wardrobe, sink, toy-sized refrigerator, and a hot plate. These objects formed a continuous line along the four walls, broken only by the door into the room. There was a narrow oblong empty space in the middle of the room and beyond the arborite table was the sole curtainless window. It had a long crack across the lower pane.

She frowned as she stared at the cracked window. What am I doing here? This is a mistake. A big mistake. What kind of home is this? A shabby little room jam-packed with junky furniture. I want to go home.

She shivered and wrapped her arms around her chest. A terrible mistake. This isn't what I planned, not at all what I imagined. This is supposed to be exciting. I am free of everyone, free to be myself, whomever I want. She looked away from the window at the room and shivered again, and a tremor travelled across her shoulders and through her back and chest and down her legs. I'll be alright. I will.

A cardboard box and a bright green knapsack sat on the table. All her belongings were in this room, sitting exactly as she had left them earlier that day when she and Rachel had moved everything from Rachel's flat. It wouldn't take much time tomorrow to unpack the box and knapsack and the black duffel bag on the floor beside the easy chair.

The easy chair was upholstered in imitation black leather. There were two clumsy strips of masking tape across the seat, hiding a long tear. She had ignored the tear when she rented the room last week, just as she had ignored the cracked window. She had been eager to find a place to live because she hated imposing on her cousin Rachel and she wanted a place of her own.

She lowered her head, burying her chin in the folds of the scarf around her neck, and closed her eyes. This will do for now. There isn't much choice. Housing is impossible to find in London and everything is so expensive. Once I'm settled, I'll find a better place to live. She opened her eyes and looked around. It'll do. I'll find something better, later.

Leaning down to the floor board, she switched on the electric heater. A faint red glow grew and gradually illuminated the bar. She stepped a little further into the room and sat on the edge of the single bed, facing the heater. This is a beginning, no matter what Rachel said. She buried her face in her hands.

"My life is filled with beginnings lately," Jenny had said to her cousin earlier that evening, as they stood in the foyer of the King's Road Theatre.

"Beginnings? What beginnings?"

Jenny looked up at the wall clock and back at Rachel.

"All these changes. You know. A new home, a new job, living all alone in a foreign country . . . "

"This isn't a foreign country. This is England!"

Jenny laughed apologetically. "It's foreign to me."

"Change is invigorating. It gives one a chance to see new things and to meet new people and new ways of being. These aren't beginnings, Jenny. Each one is a continuation of your life. With new twists, yes, but not beginnings."

Jenny thought for a moment, preparing to defend herself. "I've never worked in a hospital before. That's a beginning."

"An office in a hospital won't be much different from an office in an office tower, now, will it? Masses of women wearing uniforms and hats, rather than men in suits, that's all. Absolutely the same, really. But more interesting, I should think, to work with women all around."

"Caps, Rachel. Nurses wear caps, not hats."

"Yes, of course, that's what I meant to say."

Jenny stuffed her hands into her pockets and looked at the clock. "I've never lived alone before."

Her deepest anxiety was thrown out with deliberate casualness.

Rachel smiled. "What about the winter your parents came here to visit the relatives. You lived alone then. You looked after the house while they were away, didn't you?"

"They were only gone for three weeks. I knew they'd be back. And my sister lived just a few blocks away. It wasn't like living alone."

Rachel reached out and patted Jenny's shoulder. "Well, take it one day at a time, and before you know where you are it will be nothing extraordinary. Make it an adventure, something to enjoy and learn from. You've found a place to live. You've found employment. You are managing nicely."

"Yes. I guess so." Jenny did not sound convinced.

"You may find that you prefer to live alone." Rachel laughed, shaking her head from side to side so that her long hair flew in all directions. "That would be a shocker, wouldn't it." As her head moved, Rachel's eyes caught sight of the clock. "Look at the time. Angus is late. Where can he be? I said seven o'clock. If he's not here in a minute, we'll go in without him."

"Is he usually late?"

Rachel nodded. "It's one of his bad habits. Have you heard from Elaine?"

Jenny twisted a button on her coat. "No. I don't expect to. You know she left for Africa last week. Maybe she'll send a postcard. I don't know. She said she wants to be free. Maybe she'll send you a postcard. She doesn't want to be free of you."

Jenny lifted her head and looked around the room. I wish Rachel was here, right now. I need to talk to someone about Elaine. Coffee. That's what I need. I'll make some coffee and read for a while before going to bed.

Taking a final glance around the crowded oblong room, Jenny stood up and removed her coat and scarf. She tucked the scarf in the coat pocket and draped the coat over a hook in the empty wardrobe, moving quietly so she would not disturb the other tenants of the sleeping house. She reached beneath the sink for the dented pot, filled it with cold water, and placed it on the hot plate. Then she stood staring at the knob on the hot plate and rubbing her cold hands together. Is four hotter than one? She turned the knob through *off* to *four.*

"Or is one hotter than four?"

Look at me. I'm talking to myself. She knelt beside the duffel bag. I'm talking out loud with no one to hear but me. She undid the cord of the bag and pulled out a wrinkled flannel nightgown. Is that the first sign? Will I go crazy if I live alone? She undressed in a hurry, kneeling on the floor close to warmth from the heater. Guiding the soft flannel over her head, she slipped her arms through the sleeves and lowered the bodice around her. I want to live alone. I won't go crazy. It's absurd. Lots of people live alone and don't go crazy. I'll be quite fine. She remained crouched by the heater, rubbing her cold hands together and enjoying the warmth. This is an adventure, like Rachel said. She looked down at the creased nightgown. Here they call it a nightdress. She slid her feet into the cotton sandals that served as slippers and moved the heater closer to the bed. Whatever they call it, it isn't going to be warm enough in this freezing cold room.

After unpacking a cup and a spoon and a small jar of instant coffee from the cardboard box, she noticed the water in the pot was still cold. She checked the element. It was lifeless. She stood, puzzled, and felt a knot in her stomach. She looked around the room and fought an urge to seize the pot and the hot plate and throw them through the cracked window. She noticed an electrical cord hanging from the back of the hot plate and bent down to the wall outlet and turned it on. The element beneath the pot quickly turned from black to glowing red. The stomach knot loosened.

I can manage on my own. I don't need Elaine. Don't need anyone. Turning toward the window, she saw her reflection and paused. I wonder if anyone out there can see me standing here? Behind her image, the room was reflected in the black glass. She stared at the second-hand image of blurred furniture and the bright green of her knapsack. For all I know, I could be the only person left alive in the world.

Jenny moved closer to the window. She concentrated on trying to see beyond the glass. She could make out an outline of a row of houses, backing onto the garden behind her house. I won't think about Elaine and I will be alright. Near the end of the row, one solitary window was lit.

As soon as Angus arrived, they hurried into the theatre. The show started as they seated themselves. *The Rocky Horror Picture Show* was an uncommonly popular play. Night after night, year after year, audiences watched Frank N. Furter, a man, wearing dangerously high heels and delicious red-black lipstick. Jenny and her companions were spellbound during the performance.

Afterwards, they shared a table in a nearby pub and discussed the play over glasses of sour red wine.

"In the final scene we are handed a message, 'don't dream it, be it,' even though his own attempts to 'be it' were his downfall." Rachel tapped her fingertips on the table top. "And all the violence can't be necessary to the plot."

Jenny sipped some wine and made a face. "The moral ending is boring and it's not very original. We must pay for our pleasure, and pay heavily if we go too far. It's a common theme in literature, especially for women who dare to enjoy themselves. And what is Frank N. Furter but a womanly man?" She laughed, still feeling excitement from the outrageous play. "But what fun he had doing exactly what he pleased."

"He was inconsiderate of the feelings of everyone else. He was selfish." Angus frowned. "Selfish." One hand held the stem of his wine glass and he stared at the dark wine.

"Speaking of inconsiderate, you were thirty minutes late."

Jenny laughed as Rachel's words brought Angus' head up from his vision in the wine glass. She watched him shove a hand through his hair as he apologized. He was a prim and proper boy, as unlike his sister as two people could be.

Jenny had enjoyed their party. The conversation was always lively because they rarely agreed on anything. When Jenny and Rachel agreed on something, they could count on Angus to have a different, usually conservative, opinion. Once, she started to say, "Elaine believes . . ." and stopped herself before the words left her mouth. Elaine was gone, gone forever. There was no point in thinking about her, no point in mentioning her. It was wiser to forget her, safer to pretend Elaine had never existed.

Since London Transport ruled them, dependent as they were on buses and the Underground to get around the gigantic city, the party broke up early. At the bus stop, before they parted to go their separate ways, Jenny told Rachel that the wall meter for electricity to her room was most definitely a new thing in her life. She was pleased with herself to have thought of it. Another proof of beginnings in her life.

Rachel laughed and hugged her. "Feeding ten pence through the slot? Pretend it's a parking meter. You've used them, haven't you? Pop in the ten pee. It's simple."

Jenny chuckled at the thought of a parking meter in the hall outside her room. She turned from the dark window and opened the door of the wardrobe. Her coat looked forlorn, hanging by itself. But it'll be easy to keep this place clean and tidy, with little space and so few things. Cleaning from top to bottom will take less than an hour. She reached into the pocket of her coat and removed the handful of heavy ten-pence coins that she had been collecting and hoarding all day and evening. She closed the door and stacked the coins in three tidy piles on the bureau, beside the glossy cover of *Time Out* magazine.

She heard a faint sound. What's that? It's here, right here in my room. She looked quickly around the room, and then over at the pot. Bubbles were rushing to the surface of the water. She leaned against the bureau for a moment, giving her heartbeat a chance to slow down.

As she made coffee, the familiar smell soothed her. I shouldn't drink this. It'll keep me up. I must be feeling weak to indulge myself.

She picked up the magazine on her way to the bed, carrying the mug of steaming coffee carefully in her other hand. She made herself comfortable with the lumpy pillow propped behind her and looked at the colourful magazine cover. This is another new thing. Jenny smiled as she sipped the coffee. She could hear Rachel's voice, "A magazine is a magazine. You have magazines at home, don't you?" It was a relief to find she liked her foreign cousins, especially Rachel. Especially Rachel. She felt she had a ready-made friend in this strange place. Without Rachel and with Elaine gone, she'd be all alone.

Jenny opened the cover and leafed slowly through the pages. She had bought the magazine this afternoon at the tobacconist down the road, after she and Rachel moved everything into the room.

Rachel pointed the magazine out to her, saying, "It's our alternative magazine. It tells you what's on at the underground theatres and cinemas and has controversial articles on current issues from a leftist perspective. I found my flat in the ads at the back."

Jenny skimmed through the articles and looked at the photographs, until she arrived at the classified ads. JOBS. She skipped over that section and the next two, FLATS/ROOMS and TRAVEL. She sipped coffee and read the ads in the column titled DESTINY/SPIRITUALITY. The last section was called LONELY HEARTS.

That's what I have, a lonely heart. And it's all Elaine's fault. Getting me to come here with her and then leaving me. Abandoning me as soon as we arrived. I thought it would be different here, that we wouldn't fight all the time. How could I have been so stupid? We were wrong for each other from the beginning. That's what she said and she was right. But I'm not going to think about her. I won't!

Jenny started to read the LONELY HEARTS ads, pausing to reread one that caught her imagination.

Beginnings

>Gay woman, 31, poet, wants to meet crea-
>tive, honest, politicized woman for friend-
>ship and mutual inspiration. Box U437.

She read the ad again, and then another time. This is
definitely a liberal magazine, to have ads from dykes.
Friendship and mutual inspiration. I like the sound of that.
She stopped at another ad.

>Lesbian socialist feminist feeling down
>would like to meet a woman also conscious
>of having a lot to learn but always strug-
>gling. Over 25 please. Box U338.

This one sounds interesting too. *Always struggling.* I'm
always struggling.
Near the end of the final column, she found a third ad.

>Bi-sexual female, inexperienced, seeks attrac-
>tive lady, 20's, to bring me out of my shell.
>Photo please. Box U145.

This one wants a photo. There's no pretence. She's
looking for external beauty. But I don't have any photos
here.
She went back through the columns of ads to find the
first one. *Friendship and mutual inspiration. Creative,
honest, politicized woman.* What an intriguing choice of
words. It would be another new experience, an adventure,
perhaps a beginning, to reply to a lonely hearts ad. No
matter what Rachel says. Should I write to her? What
would Rachel say?

Jenny closed the magazine. She looked around the room, searching her mind for ways to rearrange the furniture. Holding the mug with both hands, she gulped the lukewarm coffee. It's impossible to do anything with a small room. There's only so much space. The walls are ugly. That yellow colour looks dirty. I'll buy white paint on Monday and cover it up. That will change the atmosphere of the room. I wonder if the landlord will pay for paint? Maybe a pale blue would look better. Blue's a cold colour, isn't it? I need warmth in here.

She put the magazine and empty mug on the dresser. Will the poet come here to visit me? She switched off the electric heater and overhead light. Returning to bed, she tucked herself in between the sheets and beneath four heavy blankets of man-made fibres. The only sound was the leaky tap.

Drip. Drip drip.   Drip.

She opened her eyes and looked around the dark room. I will be comfortable here. I have to put everything away and get to know the house and the people who live in the other rooms. And I'll get to know the neighbourhood.

She turned over onto her side, and closed her eyes.

Drip. Drip drip.   Drip.

The mattress sagged in the middle and she was caught in the hollow. She shifted her body and then shifted again, trying to get comfortable.

Tomorrow I will go for a walk. She imagined herself walking along streets, smiling shyly at other solitary women and women with children. The images made her feel hopeful. She turned over and pulled the covers up over her mouth and nose. Her mind started racing, leaping from thought to thought.

Beginnings

It's cold in here⠀⠀I'm freezing. Should I turn the heater on? Is it dangerous to leave it on while I'm sleeping? I could die in this bed⠀⠀no one would know⠀⠀not for days⠀⠀days⠀⠀maybe not for weeks! No⠀⠀that's absurd⠀⠀I won't die here⠀⠀And I'm not crazy to talk to myself⠀⠀to talk out loud. That's not crazy behaviour. It's like thinking inside my head only saying it out loud. It doesn't mean anything⠀⠀no

⠀⠀⠀⠀⠀⠀⠀⠀⠀Will I be able to do it to live alone? What if I can't? If I talk to myself what else will I do? Will I follow the first friendly smile? Take any opportunity to touch another woman⠀⠀to be touched? I'm scared to be alone⠀⠀*a lonely heart.* I don't want to get involved with someone because I'm scared to be by myself. That would be a mistake⠀⠀dangerous mistake. This is my chance to do anything⠀⠀whatever I want. Anything.

⠀⠀⠀I wonder what she looks like? *Gay woman poet.* Tall I bet⠀⠀with rosy cheeks. Yes⠀⠀rosy cheeks and a warm smile. Rosy cheeks⠀⠀she'll carry her poems in a grubby notebook. A special one⠀⠀with an old ribbon tied around it to hold the poems in. A red velvet ribbon. Maybe gentle blue. *Friendship and mutual inspiration.* She'll show me her poems. I'll show her mine. Poems about loving women. We'll read to one another.

⠀⠀⠀⠀⠀⠀⠀⠀⠀I don't know anyone⠀⠀not one person in this whole country. Alone⠀⠀lonely⠀⠀except Rachel. And Angus. But he's a man. I'm lucky to have Rachel⠀⠀so lucky to have a cousin here⠀⠀luckier still that she's a dyke. What are the odds of finding two dykes in one family? I am lucky⠀⠀lucky

⠀⠀⠀*Drip. Drip drip.⠀⠀Drip.*

I've got to do something about that leaky tap. Will the

landlord fix it? I can't live with this   don't have to put up
with it. I'll write to the poet and invite her here. Is she a
good poet?

I'll paint the walls and make this my home.
Home is important. I left home   left all my friends and
my family   left everyone to come here with Elaine. How
could she leave me? She didn't even give us a chance here.
It could have been different. No chance. One week and
she left   a week. That wasn't how we planned it. I don't
need her. I'll manage on my own. I'll be alright without
her. I got along before her. I don't need her don't need
anyway I have Rachel. Did she notice how much Angus
enjoyed playing Frank N. Furter at the bus stop? I think
he's a faggot. Poofter they say here. Does Rachel know? He
looked so young and carefree   *toucha toucha toucha touch*
me   what did the other people at the bus stop think of
him   with his hands perched on his hips   throwing
back his head and singing   *toucha toucha toucha touch*
me. It was the red wine. He had four glasses. Or was it
five? The wine released his true spirit. *Toucha   toucha*

If I answer the ad will she write back to me? She's an
older woman   thirty-one   but six years isn't that much
older. Would she come here to my place? I could invite her
for supper. I'll paint the room first. *Friendship and mutual*
inspiration. What would I write to her? What could I say?
If she's been politicized why does she call herself gay?
Don't politicized women call themselves lesbians?

Drip. Drip drip.   Drip.

Jenny rolled onto her back and opened her eyes. Is she
looking for a friend? Or a lover? What will Rachel say if I
answer the ad?

She imagined Rachel sitting on the edge of the bed

beside her, holding her hand and laughing. "You came here because you wanted change. You wanted to explore the world. Take risks!"

Jenny got up, switched on the overhead light and the heater, and took a pencil and small notebook from the pocket of the green knapsack. She shivered as she crossed the small room. Sitting on the edge of the bed, close to the warmth of the heater, she rearranged the blankets to cover her legs. She opened the notebook and began to write.

I sit on my single bed
in this cold bedsitting room
feel the strangeness
dingy yellow paint on the walls
strips of faded colour in the rug
the not-quite-regular beat
of the dripping tap
my few possessions
wait
          to be unpacked
                    and sorted

I read your ad

Gay woman, 31, poet
wants to meet
creative,
honest,
politicized woman
for friendship
and mutual inspiration

Freedom Fighter

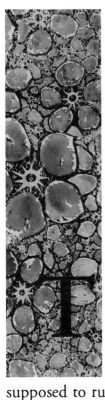

hey never come when you want one. Goddamn buses. Don't know why they bother to print schedules. Waste of good money. Buses never follow 'em. They're supposed to run every twelve minutes at rush hour. Every twelve minutes. So where the hell is it?

Rita shifted her weight from one foot to the other.

Where is that damn thing? She looked at her watch and then stared down the street. I've been waiting here for twenty-five long minutes. That bus is always late. Rotten service. The price is always going up and the service gets worse. Every January first the tickets cost more. Damned nerve they have, to up the prices.

She looked at her watch again, and then down the street. There's one! It's about time. It better be my bus. She moved the quilted shopping bag to her other hand and looked at her watch again. At this rate, it'll be seven before

I get home and eight before we eat. Damn! She squinted, trying to read the number on the approaching bus. Looks like . . . is that two numbers? A one and a five? Or is it a one and a six? It better be mine.

Rita reached into her red leather shoulder bag and pulled out a plastic bus pass. Is it the fifteen? It's got to be. It's already late and getting later every minute. How could I forget to leave the pork chops out to thaw. Supper's going to be late and I don't know what we'll have. Maybe scrambled eggs. Are there enough eggs in the fridge? She shifted from one foot to the other. I hope there's a goddamn seat. My legs are aching.

The large slow-moving bus was almost at the stop before she could read the number. A fifteen. About time. She got her pass ready to show the driver and tightened her grip on the quilted bag. As the bus glided to a stop at the curb, with a loud hissing from the hydraulic brakes, Rita moved forward impatiently. As soon as the door opened, she stepped quickly onto the bus.

Look at that. It finally gets here, after twenty-five minutes, and it's packed. Goddamn bus! I've got to sit down. This aching's unbearable. She flashed her pass in the driver's direction and started walking down the aisle, looking for a vacant seat. She saw one near the back and hurried towards it. The bus started and then stopped abruptly, throwing her backwards then forwards. She reached out for something to grab, to prevent herself from falling. Holding firmly to the back of a seat, she regained her balance and bent forward to pick up her bus pass. Where do they get these bus drivers? Goddamn heavy foot on the pedals. Someone should teach him how to drive. She continued her voyage to the vacant seat at the back of the bus.

Freedom Fighter

Before she sat down Rita slipped her red bag off her shoulder, and once she was seated she held the shoulder bag and quilted bag on her lap. A seat. What a relief. My legs feel better already.

Then she heard the noise. The THUMP THUMP THUMP of a pounding bass. What's that racket? Where's it coming from? She looked around. The young fellow beside her was sitting with his eyes closed, his feet resting on a case of beer, muffled sounds blaring out from his headphones.

Goddamn, he's going to grow up deaf. No consideration for anyone else. A crowded bus and he has his music that loud! I don't want to listen to his racket. My legs are aching and I had to stand for a half hour waiting for the damn bus and it finally comes and I get a seat and now this!

Rita reached over and tapped his arm. He opened his eyes slowly, looking first at her hand and then at her face.

She withdrew her hand. "Would you mind turning down your music, please?"

He didn't say a word before closing his eyes again.

Goddamn kids. No respect for anyone. Not even themselves. How old can he be? Nineteen? Twenty? He acts like a bad-tempered five-year-old. His father must be ashamed of him. Does he know his son acts like this in public? A half hour waiting for the damn bus and now this. I'm not putting up with it.

She tapped his shoulder, this time moving her hand away quickly. He opened his eyes and glared at Rita.

"Please. Turn down the music. It's so loud the whole bus can hear it."

"Fuck off, old bag." He gave her the finger before he closed his eyes.

OLD! He called me *old*. And he told me to fuck off. Who does he think he is? He called me an old bag and told me to fuck off. I've worked hard all day and I'm tired and my legs are aching and I still have to make supper when I get home and then do the dishes and make the lunches for tomorrow. I bet he treats his mother like this too. I'll show him an old bag! Him and his finger. I'll fuck off alright.

Rita reached into the red shoulder bag and rummaged around. She pulled out a pair of dainty manicure scissors. She tapped the young man on the shoulder. When he opened his eyes and looked at her, she looked him straight in the eye and cut the cord which connected the radio to his headphones.

He stared at her, his mouth dropping open. He didn't speak for a minute, and when he finally found the words he sounded like a whiny five-year-old. "What did you have to do that for! You can't do that! I wasn't bothering no one. What did you have to do that for?"

A woman in the seat ahead turned around. She looked at the tiny scissors in Rita's hand and then at the severed cord. "Thank you," she said softly, smiling at Rita.

Without Regrets

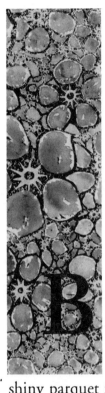

Blood everywhere. An erratic trail of bright red spots from the sink to the fridge, the fridge to the stove, the stove to the hallway. There was a line of tiny dots along the shiny parquet floor in the hall and then a few large crimson puddles. She could see a smeared red footprint outside the bedroom.

Standing in the doorway, too frightened to move, unable even to think, she stared at the bloody trail that led to the bedroom. Pain, excruciating pain, a hard knot that throbbed and cursed in all directions. Her hand moved instinctively to her body, clutching the damp skin.

Julie woke to a feeling of sticky wetness on her thigh. Had the alarm gone off? No. Awake before the alarm. What a strange dream. What was it? Red. Blood everywhere. She turned over with a quick movement and felt the belly-ache and then her hip touched a damp spot on the sheet. Noooo. The cold wetness pressed against her hip. Pain and a mess in the bed. She opened her eyes quickly, squinting at the darkness. What to do? If she could shake off her sleepiness. If she could wake up. Think. Blood on the sheets. Soaked through? Not another stain on the mattress.

Get up. Wake up. Out of bed. To the bathroom. Quickly. Move fast so the blood does not fall, does not leak out and land on the floor. How could she have forgotten her period was due? Her breasts were tender yesterday and she has been feeling anxious for the last few days.

Month after month without fail and still somehow she manages to forget.

Wetness oozed onto her thigh. She shoved back the covers, reacting, moving without thinking, leaping out of bed and running to the bathroom — a streak of naked urgency.

She sat on the toilet. Safe. No flying red drops disturbed the smooth green and white tile floor. She examined the smear of blood along her thigh. Why today? The smell of menstrual blood filled her nostrils and she felt tears starting in her gut. Noooo. It would be an effort to get through the day if she started crying now. Tears would colour the day and everything would go wrong.

She busied herself at the bathroom sink, rushing although barely awake, soaking the face cloth with warm water, washing blood from her pubic hair and from her thighs and hips, then placing a thick pad between her legs. She tried to calm herself and take charge of the situation. Be calm. Ignore the back ache. Don't give in to the anxiety.

She held the pad with one hand, hobbling awkwardly
to the bedroom to get underpants to hold the pad in
place. Once the snug black cotton underpants were on,
holding the pad securely against her body, she dressed
herself in the pale blue leggings and T-shirt she liked to
use as pyjamas. She pulled the blood-stained sheet off the
bed, deliberately ignoring the spot of red on the mattress,
tucked the sheet under her arm and went into the kitchen.

Dropping the sheet on the floor, she took the milk
carton from the fridge and poured herself a glass. This was
not the best way to start the day, but she would not let it
get her down. Noooo. It was mind over body. She would
rise above it and have a satisfying day at work. She would.
Somehow. Fighting an urge to cry, struggling to hold back
the tears, she swallowed a pain pill with some milk.

It had to be either a physiological response to the
hormone levels in her body or a learned emotional response. Which? Every month when her period started,
she speculated about it. She could never decide. If she
understood what happened, if she knew the cause, surely
she could overcome the urges to weep and the feelings of
despair. She hated to think this was an emotional response, hated to think she got *that way* once a month. Was
she a victim of biology? A victim. Noooo. Not her.

She filled the sink with cold water and submerged the
bloody sheet, then she turned on the coffee maker. What
did it matter! The first day of her period tried and tested
her inner resources every thirty days, whatever the cause.

She took a long drink of milk. She would have preferred to stay home for the first day. She imagined herself
enjoying an unstructured day, hours of indulging herself
and doing nothing much except watching TV and maybe

repotting plants or baking cookies or spending the day in bed with a good book. A day of doing what she felt like doing, taking as much time as she needed, and resting in between.

She adjusted the pad in the crotch of her underpants. The thick wedge between her thighs bothered her every month, irritating her beyond words. Was it because she had never accepted her periods? Who would want to accept this. It was a bother, carrying pads everywhere and having to remember to visit a bathroom every half hour or so the first day and still managing to stain at least one pair of underpants each period. The blood was impossible to get out. There were already two stains on the mattress, which was a mere three years old. She had tried to scrub the stains away. She used hand soap and dish soap and then Mr. Clean and finally an S.O.S pad but nothing removed the blood.

Leaning on the stove, she took another long drink of milk and emptied the glass. She stared out the open window and felt close to tears again. The lilac bushes along the fence were in full bloom and the sweet scent was strong in the early morning air. She hated her period, it was true, hated this monthly tyranny and longed for it to end.

She looked up at the cloudless sky. It would be another hot and sunny day. She loved the humid summer hotness. That was one good thing about today. Focus on the good things. Find the strength to get through the day. Tomorrow would be better. The second day always was.

She decided she would go in early and get a head start at work. What was happening today? Using both hands, she massaged the small of her back. Myra was expecting the report and it was nearly finished, just needed some statistics and another read-through to tighten the writing. Again, she felt tears starting in her gut. She turned away from the window, moving quickly, and poured coffee into a mug. She'd do that first thing, work on the report before the others arrived. If she could get the report finished it would make the rest of the day easier.

She poured milk into the mug, turning the black coffee a creamy brown. The phone company. Someone was coming in to install a new phone system. How could she have forgotten? He'd need to know where the main box was and where to install the phones and which ones were to ring. He was bound to have other questions and need information she couldn't anticipate. He would be interrupting her all morning.

If the installer was a woman, Julie could tell her that this was the first day of her period and the phone woman would understand. She returned the milk carton to the fridge. But it wouldn't be a woman. The phone company always sent a man, a young one in jeans and safety boots with heavy gadgets hanging from his leather belt. What did the phone company do with the men as they aged?

She sipped the coffee. Why did her period have to start today, when she had so much to do? How would she get the report finished? It would be unbearable if Myra was angry today. Myra had been displeased last week when Julie was late coming back from lunch. Myra was a workaholic, no question about it, and demanded the same dedication from everyone. Myra was, Julie suspected, often disappointed. No one met her high expectations, not even her own self.

She looked at the clear blue sky. At forty-four, isn't it time for menopause? She read somewhere that recent research indicates women start menopause around thirty-four or thirty-five. Maybe it was already happening to her, had been for years. She couldn't tell. She still had these periods every month. And the cramps. The backaches. The anxiety. Stained underpants. Thick damp pads. Stained mattress.

Menopause was a word that frightened her. All she knew were rumours of hot flashes and deep depressions and bizarre behaviour. What would it really be like? Surely it would be better than this each month. Or would hot flashes disturb her moods? Would it be worse to waken in a hot sweat and have to change sopping wet sheets in the middle of the night?

What about the bizarre behaviour?

Last month, when Julie said she was longing for her periods to end, Marianne had said she wasn't looking forward to it because her mother went crazy during menopause.

"What do you mean, crazy?" Julie had heard stories over the years about women acting crazy, but no one ever said what the craziness was about.

There was silence for a moment then Marianne said, "Well, that's when she started drinking every day, during the change. She'd have sherry before supper and wine after supper and some days she didn't bother making supper at all. We had to do it if we wanted to eat. She'd sit in her bedroom with the door closed and cry. We could hear her. It was horrible."

"But what was happening in the rest of her life? Your father was never home, was he? He's married to his job. He never has time for anyone. She must have been awfully lonely."

"Maybe she was. You know Dad's always busy. I don't know what he's going to do when he retires next year. Back then my oldest sister was going to university in Waterloo and she'd always been close to Mom. My brother was in Alberta working in construction and I know she used to worry about him, but she never heard from him. He's always been like that. He never phoned and never wrote. Sharee was gone too, living with her boyfriend, that dumbbell she married. Marcie and I were in high school but we had our own lives."

Julie sipped coffee. She had a job she liked and a full life and close friends. She wouldn't turn to drink to console herself. She wouldn't need to. Could the hot flashes be any worse than this day of tyranny, month after month and year after year for thirty-three years. Menopause had to be better. Hot flashes wouldn't be worse than this, they just couldn't be.

She reached down to adjust the thick pad. And menopause wouldn't last thirty-three years!

What sort of hell had Marianne's mother gone through, that drove her to alcohol and the bedroom and solitary tears? No one went in. No arms held her. Her family went on with their lives on the other side of the bedroom door. She must have been lonely. Scared. Her children were leaving home. Maybe she felt old. She had no one to talk to. Isolated at home. It wasn't menopause that made her inconsolable. It was her life.

"One time, when he was complaining about something or other, she picked up a plate of hot food and threw it at him. No one said anything. Not even my father, for once. She'd never done anything like that before. He was always complaining, constantly, about everything, you know how he does, but she'd never thrown anything at him before. That was scary."

Frightening for your mother, too. Julie didn't share her thoughts with Marianne. It was a wonder, as far as Julie was concerned, that Marianne's mother hadn't done something like that years before and it was a wonder she hadn't thrown something more violent than hot food. It always upset Julie to be around Marianne's parents. Marianne's father treated her mother like a naughty, no, like a disobedient child with some kind of learning disability. "Did you remember to get my shirts from the cleaner?" he would ask, saying each word clearly and in a tone that implied it would be a miracle if she had.

Julie had to resist a strong urge to place herself between them, had to ignore her impulse to protect Marianne's mother. She wanted to scream at him, "LOOK AFTER YOUR OWN FUCKING SHIRTS!" Instead, she avoided visiting Marianne's family, without ever giving Marianne an explanation. She feared the truth would jeopardize their friendship. Marianne adored her domineering father and usually sided with him against her mother.

A shower — that's what she needed to make her feel clean and fresh. She placed the empty coffee mug on the kitchen table and returned to the bathroom.

Julie stood beneath the full spray of hot water, not moving, taking deep breaths and inhaling the moist warm air. Was Marianne's mother's depression connected to menopause? She had so many other reasons to be depressed.

Julie coughed and the sound echoed in the small steamy room. Her period had lasted only three days last month, rather than the usual five. Must be menopause.

Could it be? Could it be close, at last?

She'd read a short newspaper article that said research-
ers believe menopause comes earlier for women who have
never been pregnant. Millions of women went through
menopause every year, had been going through menopause for hundreds of years, maybe thousands of years,
and scientists were just beginning to do research. She read
somewhere else that they had only recently started to
study menstruation, as well. That's what happens when
you let men take charge of things. They ignore women.

She would tell Myra that it was the first day of her
period and that she would try to get the report finished.
But, if it didn't get done, it didn't get done. Tough. She
wouldn't say *tough* to Myra. Not unless Myra drove her to
it with one of her sarcastic comments.

Julie started to cry, small contained sobs that she could
barely hear under the shower. Cry, she told herself. Let it
out and get it over with. Bending forward, covering her
face with her hands, she sobbed and sobbed and sobbed.
She stood up and opened her mouth and howled. The
noises sounded loud and painful.

After a few minutes, she turned around and held her
face up to the hot water. Warm. That felt better. Julie
sniffed as she reached for the soap. Would she have hot
flashes? What would it be like? Like the way she sweated
on humid summer afternoons? So much of life is surrounded by myths and half-lies. She would ask her
mother. Her mother had had a hysterectomy when she
was thirty-nine, younger than Julie was now, and had
taken a hormone drug for years afterwards. Was it
estrogen? She remembered her mother saying that the
hysterectomy had been a relief, because she didn't have to

worry about getting pregnant any more and didn't have the bother of periods. Pregnant! Julie chuckled. That wasn't a concern. No way.

She lathered the soap over her body, scrubbing with concentration. It was going to be a busy day and she'd have to go to the bathroom umpteen times to pull a soiled pad away from her underpants — always hoping she hadn't leaked through to her underpants and, if she had, hoping it hadn't gone through to her trousers. Her only pleasure was the feel of a fresh new pad, but it was all too soon replaced by that unsettling wet sensation.

She reached between her legs and created a generous lather in her pubic hair. Tonight her pubic hair would be matted with dried blood and clots. She would want a bath as soon as she got home.

It was the smell that disturbed her, more than any-thing. The pad soaked with menstrual fluid gave off an odour. And, after a couple of days, her pubic area itched all the time, as if the pad prevented oxygen from getting to that area of her body. Pads. She hated them.

She remembered all too clearly the humiliation of buying pads when she was in her teens. The druggist would hurry to put the bulky box in a paper bag as soon as she set it on the counter, as if it was something to be hidden, before ringing up the sale on the cash register. She avoided looking at him and prayed she wouldn't blush. Walking home, the large bag gripped tightly in her hand, she was sure everyone knew what she was carrying, espe-cially every boy she passed on the street.

She felt different now. She never cared if men recog-nized the box, didn't mind if boys waited behind her and saw the box sitting on the counter. Young women clerks were equally as casual, treating the transaction like any other. The box of pads could have been toothpaste or a bottle of vitamin C tablets for all they cared. No one rushed to conceal it in a plastic carry bag. Times had changed.

She turned around and around, letting the water wash over her and away. She would get through this day by living in the moment. She would not worry about the rest of the day. She stepped out of the shower and wrapped a towel around her body. She had to move quickly, to get a pad in place before menstrual blood ran down her thighs and dripped on the floor. She was encumbered, bound for the next few days. There was no escape. Except, maybe, except menopause. How much longer would she have to wait? Two years? Four years?

Once the pad was in place and held by a fresh pair of underpants, beige cotton this time, she towel-dried her body. Trying to position the pad to catch the flow no matter how she moved — sitting, standing, bending, walking — was guesswork. And she constantly wondered if it was time to change the pad. Her timing was usually off. The monthly experience, year after year, had not made her an expert.

Menopause could not be any worse than this. Surely it would only be an improvement. She threw the damp towel over the rack. Menopause would mean she couldn't have children. She didn't know if she could have children. She had never tried to get pregnant, had never wanted a child, but she always believed she had the choice. Menopause ended the possibility of choice. No children from this body. Never ever.

Such a thought! If she hadn't had children by age forty-four, was she likely to start now? She chuckled. Noooo.

She brushed her hair, looking around the room at the bathroom scales, the striped pink towels, the cracked tube of toothpaste, looking everywhere but at the mirror. Would menopause change her body? Make her breasts sag and her vagina dry up?

Better hurry and get going if she wanted an early start on the day. She put the brush on the shelf. She'd wear something that would make her feel extra special today. What? The blue cotton trousers, they were loose, and the short-sleeved yellow striped shirt. That would do it. She bent down and reached for plastic-wrapped pads in the cabinet beneath the sink.

She would pamper herself. She would go out for lunch, alone, to the restaurant around the corner, the pricey one with fresh flowers on each table. She'd go, even if the report wasn't finished, and have a bowl of frothy café au lait. Yes. She would take care of herself. And she would order some comfort food for lunch, cream of cauliflower soup and maybe rice pudding for dessert.

Julie turned to the naked figure in the mirror and studied the solemn face and slightly swollen breasts and then looked at the two handfuls of pads. She had to talk to someone, had to find women with the truth about menopause. If she knew what to expect she would be alright.

Elle-même With Waves

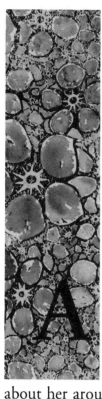ll day at work she wants to masturbate. Sitting in the small, glass-enclosed booth, she reads a novel by Margaret Laurence. She stops and stares into space and thinks about her aroused body. She wonders why she is aroused. It can't be the novel. It isn't that sort of book. And then a customer appears at the window, and she has to attend to that.

She is accustomed to interruptions. When the flow of customers is constant she puts the book aside, using a creased bus transfer to mark her place. A few times during the lunch hour there is a small line-up of drivers waiting to pay. She is never flustered. It is a simple and speedy transaction: read the meter, take the money, Thank you, count the change, give the change, You're welcome, Next please. She says "You're welcome" as she hands back the change, even when the customer does not say "Thanks."

She is no longer surprised at the number of people who turn away without a word.

The process is slowed when a customer pays with plastic, but it is not a significant delay. She is methodical and the steps are well-known. She has even learned to discreetly check the customer's signature with the one on the back of the plastic card. She is quick and tactful. Any hint of mistrust makes people defensive and angry.

She likes watching people and sometimes plays a game with herself, appraising the appearance of the driver to see if she or he suits the make and model of the car. Today she isn't interested in the drivers or their cars. She isn't even very interested in the novel. She wants to be at home, playing with her aroused body.

She rests her chin in the cup of her hand and strokes her cheek bone with her longest finger. Aroused, for no good reason that she can think of, and has been from the moment she woke up. Not that she needs a reason to be aroused, she decides as she smiles at a woman customer. It is a gift to be enjoyed, the sensual shape and feel of her body.

The customer smiles back. "It's cold today."

She nods at the woman as she counts the change to herself, sixteen fifty, seventeen, eighteen, and two makes twenty. "And the temperature's going to drop tonight."

The customer takes her change. "Thank you. Is that a good book?"

"You're welcome." She shifts slightly on the padded seat and feels the wetness in her pants. "I think it's her best."

"I'll have to read it. Have a good day."

"You have a good day and come again." She watches

the customer — short blonde hair, jeans, and a stylish black leather jacket — walk back to her car, a grey Honda Civic. A dyke, no question about it. The woman drives the Civic onto the street and honks twice. She laughs and waves and then hands change to the next customer. She forgets to say "You're welcome" to him.

In the late afternoon, a couple of hours before the end of her shift, she starts thinking about being at home. She yearns to be in the privacy of her living room, to close the curtains and turn on the stereo. She wants to put her hands in her pants, touch the sticky wetness, slide her fingers up and down, hold her fingers under her nose. Sweet smell.

The minutes pass slowly. She can't read anymore, can't concentrate on the printed words. She is, she supposes, too excited, too delightfully distracted by her body. She crosses her legs and flexes the muscles in her thighs.

When the shift ends, she counts the money in her cash drawer, hoping it will balance with the receipts. She is rushing and that is when she is likely to make mistakes and have to do it all over again. It's a wondrous relief when the totals match the first time. Everything is in her favour. Free, at last, to please herself. She leaves quickly, barely acknowledging the arrival of the fellow who works the evening shift.

At home, a short bus ride later, she lays the novel on a chair and immediately begins preparations for a bath. It will be a sensual bath, slow and leisurely. She needs music. An album? A cassette? Her hand reaches for a cassette, almost involuntarily, intuitively, taking her favourite, the one taped for her by her sister, an eclectic combination of women's voices — Buffy St-Marie, Joan Armatrading,

Shirley Eikhard, Meg Christian, k.d. lang, Marianne Faithfull, Fabienne Thibeault, Tracy Chapman, Rita MacNeil, and Emmy Lou Harris.

She likes that word, *eclectic*, she thinks as she crouches beside the pink tub. Placing the plug in the drain, turning on the taps, holding a capful of Spring Green Vitabath *gelée* under the forceful water, she hums. Eclectic evokes an image of bright sparks flying in all directions. Sparks! That's what she needs.

She takes two vanilla candles from the kitchen table and places them on either side of the tub, humming as she moves. One beside the cold water tap and one beside the hot water tap, then she lights the candles and turns off the overhead light. Yes, yes, YES!

She sings loudly with the music, pulling off her clothes, dancing to the beat, stripping slowly, dropping each piece in an untidy pile on the bathroom floor. The darkened and fragrant room feels warm and secluded. Naked, she kneels on the bath mat to watch the tub fill with clouds of white bubbles. She hums and plays with her pubic hair, gathers the strong sticky black hairs and twists them gently around and around her fingers. The tugging of hair and skin touches a deeper spot. Her fingers become wet and soft.

She turns off the taps and steps into the hot foamy water, easing her body down until she rests, stretched out, submerged to her chin, savouring the relaxing heat. Her voice trembles slightly, in unison with Buffy's, as she reaches for the high notes. She touches herself beneath the water, caressing round breasts, pebble nipples, fingertips bold and long, fingerprints recognize, thumbs and fingers skim along the curve of her belly to her pubis, dancing, beating softly at her vaginal opening, one finger in, then two, soon in and in and in. Tempting and teasing her clitoris with light touch becoming firm and purposeful. Soon, soon. Not yet. And then.

The orgasm is a rush of warmth, waves, release, relief. She rests with closed eyes and soothed body, grinning.

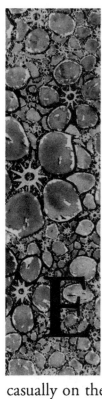

Little Scraps
and Nothingnesses

mily sits on a wooden kitchen chair close to the large window, looking out at the bare trees and heavy sky. She balances an open book on her lap and her hands rest casually on the unread pages. She is worrying about the dark clouds.

During breakfast, Willa said an overcast sky was ideal for catching fish.

She turns to Willa. "Do you think it will rain?"

Willa is reading, stretched full-length on the ancient sofa. After a moment, she looks up from the book. "Did you say something?"

Emily laughs. When Willa gets her hands on a good book she becomes totally absorbed in it. "Yes I did. I said, do you think it will rain?"

Willa looks beyond Emily, through the window. "It could. It looks like rain, doesn't it. But that wind may blow the rain clouds away. The fish don't care about rain, but that's an east wind and they'll disappear if it keeps up."

"It's a cold and bitter wind, whatever the direction. If it rains, Wil, you'll get chilled to the bone out there."

But Willa is reading again, lost to the world around her. Emily turns back to the scene on the other side of the window. The sky is hidden by dark clouds and the lake is murky grey.

During the past week, early winter winds have stripped the few remaining leaves from the maple and birch trees along the far shore of the lake. Emily mourns for the trees, for their loss and exposure, but she knows it is inevitable. She can do nothing, the trees can do nothing, except adapt — winter is on its inescapable way. The bare trees are part of a cycle, the change from one season to the next.

It is better, she decides, to focus on the piles of gorgeous leaves covering the ground beneath the bare trees. What a relief to feel like running through them, to want to throw her arms in the air and kick her feet high and scatter leaves in every direction. This image of herself, childlike and spontaneous, makes her smile.

For more than a year she had been numb. How long was it? Eighteen months? Two years? It felt like endless despair, day after day, stretching on forever. Unable to value each distinct season, unable to feel good about the changes in her life. To feel good. She thought about those words, repeating them in her mind. *To feel good.* She does feel good. Now. The months of despair and indecision are behind her. Now she feels excitement about herself and her life.

But still, she wants to understand that dismal period. It haunts her. Her mind often goes back, remembering scenes and emotions and searching for reasons, for clarity, for insight. Yet it is a fruitless search. She has questions and more questions but no answers.

Her eyes focus on the murky lake, then look inward at the main room of the cottage. The room isn't bright the way it is on sunny days, but it is filled with natural light from three walls of windows. The pine walls have a golden sheen that make her feel warm and cosy, make her want to reach out and press her fingertips along the dark honey lines and trace the knot-holes. And she approves of the furniture. Each piece, sturdy and well-worn, suits the room. Isn't it just like Sheila to cover the fourth wall, the windowless one, with lesbian and feminist posters. So typical of Sheila to decorate this cottage with symbols of her politics.

Emily smiles again as she thinks about her friend. There is no one in the whole world like Sheila. She expresses her emotions as she feels them and never pretends or hides behind politeness. *This is who I am.* That's what Sheila says to the world. *Accept me or take off!* And her politics are very much part of her life.

Emily feels a burst of good feelings every time she recalls the day a few weeks ago when she told Sheila that she was going to try to paint again.

"That's the best news!" Sheila had reached out and taken Emily's hand. "Hey, I've got an idea. Why don't you go up to my cottage for a week or two. Just the two of you. Get away and relax a little before you start your new job. See if you can paint there. It has great atmosphere and you deserve a holiday."

Emily squeezed Sheila's hand and looked at Willa.

Willa grinned and nodded. "That's not a bad idea. If

you want to, I'm willing. I have a month of leave owing me. Let's take a vacation."

"Thank you," Emily said to Sheila, feeling proud of herself for making the decision quickly and easily. "It's a great idea. You're right. We need a holiday. Thank you. Thank you!"

Sheila laughed. "You're welcome. You're welcome. But kid, as payment I want your first painting."

Emily feels tears gathering in the corners of her eyes. She shifts her body, crossing one leg over the other, and turns to look at the grey lake. She sniffs quietly, and wishes she didn't feel emotional about every little thing. She wants to be in touch with her feelings, but she is also embarrassed about displaying emotion. A contradiction. She sniffs once more and then clears her throat. Another contradiction.

Today she is going to paint, the first painting since she left high school. And then she is going to give it to Sheila, to thank her for her friendship, to thank her for sharing the cottage with them, and to ask her forgiveness for the day Emily wanted to slap her although she never confessed that shameful impulse to Sheila.

What will she paint? She has been planning this day and looking forward to it with increasing excitement, but without knowing what she will paint. How will she even start?

Emily glances back at Willa. Wil had changed her position and is curled up at the far end of the sofa, leaning toward the table lamp, transfixed by her book. Willa is a bookworm. Yucky word, worm, to apply to a beautiful woman enjoying words written by another woman.

She considers interrupting Willa again, thinks about

going over and kissing her on the cheek. She imagines Willa looking up, reluctantly, and smiling at her. So what if it rains and Willa gets wet and chilled. She is, after all, an adult and able to make her own decisions. Emily is not her mother, is not responsible for her. And anyway, it is a waste of time to worry or to take responsibility for Willa's choices. Willa is determined to go fishing today, no matter the weather. It is beyond Emily's control. Not that she wants to control Willa. But she wants to protect Willa and keep her from harm. As if she could.

It would be a better use of her energy to think about how she will spend the day while Willa is away fishing. A whole day of painting, of nothing else to do but paint without interruption. And she is going to keep at it until she produces something that pleases her, even if it means using all the sheets of paper, every last piece of thick cotton paper although each sheet cost five dollars. She is going to have something to give to Sheila when they return to the city.

What will she do if it rains and Willa decides to cancel the fishing trip?

What will she do if she can't think of anything to paint?

What will she do if . . . The sound of an engine interrupts her thoughts.

Both women turn toward the screen door which overlooks the narrow dirt road. Emily stands up and places her book on the chair. Willa blows her a kiss. They grin at one another and, without a word, Emily follows Willa out of the cottage. A van pulling a boat on a trailer drives up beside their blue Toyota, leaving a trail of dust in the air. They walk side by side, across the grass to the dirt road and the van. Emily notices that Willa is carrying the book, a finger marking her place.

There is temporary chaos as people climb out of the van — Willa's mother Margery, her father George, aunt Edna, sister Ruth, sister Marion, brother Joe and his wife Solange. The seven newcomers stand on the grass admiring the cottage, everyone talking at once about the location and the view and the size of the cabin.

Willa leads the chattering group into the main room. "Tea?" she inquires and when no one answers she puts the book on the counter, slipping a knife between the pages to keep her place, and fills the kettle with water. She places the kettle on the stove, twists the knob to on, and turns to her father. "You found the cottage without any trouble?"

"Emily's directions were clear."

Her father turns and walks away, disappearing into the bathroom. Marion pulls her aunt over to the window to admire the view. Willa shows her mother the new fishing reel. Emily explains to Ruth and Solange that they borrowed the cottage from a friend, Sheila.

Joe's voice calls across the room, interrupting their conversations. "Did you remember to bring the flashlight, Solange?"

There is a feeling of controlled excitement in the crowded cottage. Everyone is pleased to be away from the city and looking forward to a day of fishing. It is beyond Emily's ability to understand how a fishing trip could inspire this excitement, but she appreciates the feeling if not the cause. She is living with excitement herself.

Emily looks at Ruth, who is studying the posters that cover the windowless wall. Willa's family knows they are partners, lovers, companions — Emily can never decide

which label suits them — but nobody talks about it. Ruth
is the sister who seems the most liberal, the most open to
different ways of being, and the happiest in her own life.
What will Ruth think of the poster that advertises a dance
for lesbians? The one that advertises a conference for
caregivers of people with AIDS?

"Do you think it will rain?"

"No," Ruth says, turning away from the posters to look
at Emily. "It won't rain today. Isn't this a dear spot for a
vacation. Does your friend rent it out?"

Emily wonders if Ruth knows, or is she simply hoping
to prevent rain by denying the possibility. "No, not that I
know of. She says she doesn't need the money and can't be
bothered with the problems. She lets friends borrow it
from time to time and she uses it herself whenever she
can. She loves being in the country."

George returns from the bathroom. "Let's get going.
Let's get the boat in the water and load it."

Willa and Ruth and Marion and Joe follow their father
across the room.

Emily watches through the screen door while George
gives instructions and the four younger ones lift the sleek
silver boat from the trailer and carry it across the grass and
past the stately weeping willow to the dock. Once the
silver boat is floating in the water, beside Sheila's battered
green boat, Willa ties it to the small dock.

Emily walks outside with Margery, Edna, and Solange,
and stands beside Willa, watching the others open the van
and carry supplies to the boats: fishing poles, reels, tackle
boxes, a minnow pail, armfuls of faded orange life preserv-
ers, flashlights, a net, a couple of thermos bottles, plastic
containers of sandwiches and banana cake, and cape-

shaped rubber raincoats.

Emily watches Ruth tuck the yellow and green rain-coats under a seat in Sheila's old boat. Someone else predicts it may rain, she thinks with satisfaction.

"Where's my vest? Did you forget it? Solange?"

It is an indication of the depth of Emily's inner tranquillity that she does not tighten her lips, that she does not have to suppress a sarcastic comment, that she can hear and almost ignore Joe's demands on Solange.

Willa turns to Emily. "Sure you won't come with us?"

They discussed this yesterday, if Emily would go fishing. They have discussed it, off and on, for more than a week, ever since Willa decided to invite her family on a fishing trip. Willa could not understand why anyone would refuse a chance to go fishing. But Emily said no, firmly, each time Willa mentioned it. She is lacking any desire to catch fish, lacking any wish to spend hours in a small boat in the middle of a lake. It was easy to say no to the fishing trip, but difficult to say no to Willa.

"No, Wil, thanks just the same." Emily smiles and rests her fingertips on Willa's forearm. "I want to paint. If nothing else, I owe Sheila. But I hope you have a good time. And do try to stay warm and dry."

"We will," Ruth says to Emily. She is sitting in the old green boat, fiddling with something in the tackle box. "Say goodbye, Willa, and put on your life preserver and get in the boat. We'll bring you back a pickerel, Emily, for supper, so have that frying pan ready."

Emily chuckles. She likes Willa's older sister and her high spirits. "I'll be waiting." But secretly, she wouldn't admit this even to Willa, she hopes the pickerel will evade the humans and their fancy lures. She would be content to have hamburgers for supper.

She stands on the dock, shivering slightly in the cold wind, watching and waving as the two boatfuls of people row across the lake. The old green boat follows the smart silver one around the peninsula, and then everyone is gone from sight. She turns away, crossing her arms over her chest and massaging her cold shoulders. The yellow sweatshirt is not enough protection, not adequate in this wind.

The kettle is whistling noisily when Emily enters the empty cottage. She makes a pot of tea and sits on the sofa.

Returning to the city in a few days is going to be a shock, a readjustment after two weeks in the cottage. Emily wants to stay. She could be happy living here, forever content. She loves the quietness and isolation. She is able to watch the sky as the sun rises each morning, without the barriers of city buildings. Away from the distraction of city lights, she can see the stars and follow the phases of the moon on cloudless nights. She never misses the city voices of cars, trucks, buses, motorcycles, and people. She does not yearn for the perpetual city motion.

The notes and trills of sparrows from the stand of pine trees behind the cottage release seeds of adrenalin throughout her body. "Listen to those birds," she says to Willa at least twice a day. Sometimes she runs across the room and throws her arms around Willa. It is the only way she knows to express the surge of joy.

Emily is content in this peaceful cottage, close to water and protected by mature trees. It would be heaven to own a cottage like this one. In her ideal life, the one she plans in her daydreams, she and Willa rent an apartment in the city and own a country place for weekends and holidays. Nothing fancy, a simple dwelling hidden from the rest of the world. A haven, a place to feel safe with Willa.

She notices the stout brown teapot on the counter and remembers the tea. As she walks to the counter she hears the high-pitched whine of an engine. She turns and watches a speed boat race through the water, leaving behind waves that bounce against the dock with loud slapping sounds. She pours a cup of tea and adds extra milk to dilute the strong black brew while keeping an eye on the two boys in the boat. Neither one is wearing a life jacket. Moving closer to the window, holding the warm mug carefully with both hands, she watches the boat disappear around the peninsula. Foolish kids. The young take life for granted. They believe, if they bother to think about it at all, that they will live forever so they take unnecessary risks.

She turns to look at the sofa and wishes Willa was still sitting there, enthralled with her book. If it starts to rain, surely they will give up the fishing trip and come back to shore.

What will she do all day by herself? It is peaceful here, but too quiet. Even the sparrows are silent this morning. She resists the temptation to race outside and stand on the dock, yelling, WILLA!WILLA! She turns to the scene beyond the window and sips the strong lukewarm tea. She is going to paint.

She is preparing for a new phase in her life, yet she feels inner peace. She trusts herself, trusts that everything will work out. There is no place in her newly-found sense of purpose for twinges of anxiety.

There are moments when she feels there is more for her to know. The elusive sensations come at the oddest times, when she least expects it. Like this morning, when she was looking through the suitcase for her yellow sweatshirt. The feeling came over her without warning and vanished just as quickly, before she could find the words to describe what was happening. Each time, it leaves her feeling disoriented.

She had been tempted to mention it a few weeks ago, when she and Willa were discussing *déjà vu*. But what could she say? It was not like having been there before, not a flashback. It was more a sense of now. Or something still to come. Like a premonition. No, it was not a premonition. What was it?

She makes fun of herself, as she often does when something cannot be explained or analyzed. Maybe it was vertigo. She laughs out loud. Can she be mistaking a dizzy spell for a psychic experience? Those surreal moments, whatever they are, are not important. Except they started during the months of depression. Is that significant?

What is important is to understand where the depression came from in the first place. She turns, as always, to analysis. The depression didn't start at a precise moment or on a particular day. When she looks back she can't even identify the month. It started slowly and grew gradually.

Most of those months are already a blur, except for isolated incidents. Like the time she threw the mug.

Did she have to live through those painful months to reach this point? If only she could understand why it had happened, surely it would never happen again. Never again would she wander aimlessly in a forest of innumerable decisions, floundering in the tangled undergrowth of her emotions, unable to determine any clear direction. North, west, south, east. All directions took her in circles, leading her only deeper into pain and terror.

Emily was almost thirty when she decided her life lacked purpose. Everything bored her: her job, her friends, Willa, herself. The daily activities that filled her life had a predictable monotony and the routines were irritating. During the cold winter months before she turned thirty, she was mildly depressed. She preferred to stay home and never go outside. She often ignored the ringing phone because she did not want to talk to anyone. She told herself it was the January blues and the February doldrums. Everyone felt low at this time of year. It was normal to feel depressed when the temperature stayed below freezing and outdoor movement was impossible because of the penetrating cold and the treacherous snow and ice. The days were frigid and brief. The nights were long and dark.

She tried to keep the depression to herself, although a voice within her longed to talk to someone. When friends and co-workers asked, in the automatic way of greeting, "How are you," she usually responded by saying, "Not bad," or "I'm surviving." What else could she say? No one seemed to notice that her replies were guarded. No one asked for more information.

She was bored. Emily recognized that much. She worked all day at a job that bored her, had worked in the same boring place for nine years. Every weekday morning she left the apartment at 7:30 and caught a bus to work. Every weekday afternoon she left work at 4:00 and caught another bus home. Before supper she exercised in front of the television. That year she watched reruns of *Soap* as she twisted and bent and stretched her body. Afterwards she ran through Beechwood Cemetery, a short run of twenty or twenty-five minutes. During the winter months there were many days when she could not run. In the evenings and on weekends she watched television with Willa, read novels, occasionally went to a movie or a women's dance or a dinner party with Willa and sometimes with Sheila. Friday evenings she shopped for groceries. Saturday mornings she and Willa cleaned the apartment.

She wanted something more in her life, some kind of meaningful change. She couldn't go on like this, year after year. But what did she want? She only knew she could not bear to think of herself in ten years still doing the same things and looking back on this life.

In March, as the temperature started to rise and the snow and ice melted, she had every reason to feel better. Spring was on the way. But she felt worse.

There was one good week during a warm spell in April. The sun shone every day and people started wearing brightly-coloured summer clothes. Looking out the bus window on her way home from work, she saw white and purple crocuses in the grass on Parliament Hill and she felt her spirits rise.

She decided to talk to Sheila over lunch. She didn't tell Sheila she was feeling desperate because she worried that would sound melodramatic and self-indulgent. She said, instead, that she had been feeling depressed lately.

"I've noticed," Sheila said. "Don't let it get you down. It's tough turning thirty. Poor kid. It's hard on everyone. Hang in there and you'll be okay. It'll pass. We all go through it and we all get through it."

Turning thirty. Emily did not feel better after talking to Sheila, but she had a new idea to consider. Did her depression have anything to do with turning thirty?

She had worked hard for years, first in school and now
in her job, but when she looked back she felt she had
nothing to show except a boring job and a boring life. Did
she feel this way because she was turning thirty? Thirty
was a milestone. What had she accomplished?

She phoned Willa at work during the afternoon coffee
break.

"Willa? I need to tell you something. I've been kinda
depressed lately."

"Yeah, you're telling me. You've been dragging yourself
around. You've decided to talk about it?"

"I don't know. I don't know what's wrong. I don't know
why I feel this way."

"It doesn't matter why. You always worry about why.
Don't. Just do something about it. Look for another job.
You hate that job. You need to take control of your life."

"Maybe. I have been thinking about looking for another job."

"That's it, but don't just think. Do something."

"But I don't know what to do."

"Sure you do. Look for another job. That's a start. And
while you're at it why don't you start painting again.
You've talked about it enough."

Painting? Emily dismissed the idea. Her country scenes
had won praise from her art teacher in high school. But
that was a lifetime ago. When she had moved to the city
after high school, she found city landscapes did not inspire
her. She didn't have any painting equipment. And anyway,
she didn't have time to paint.

She tried to talk to her supervisor about her job and
her future. He assured her that her work was satisfactory.
She was, he said, management material. But she had to get

a university degree. He was taking his own advice and kept her in his office for most of the afternoon, talking about his course in Human Resources and complaining about his boss and bragging about his new car.

When she was finally able to escape, she sat at her desk with her face in her hands. *Turning thirty. Find a new job. Paint. Management material.* Talking to the people around her didn't help so she decided to stop talking. Maybe there was nothing anyone could do. Perhaps this was a natural crisis and she could only wait it out.

Emily's thirtieth birthday came and went but nothing changed. She was bitterly disappointed. She had hoped for a sudden transformation but she actually felt worse.

Nothing satisfied Emily. That's what Willa said to her one day, yelled at her, after Emily had been depressed for months.

"What do you expect me to do! Nothing satisfies you. Nothing! You sit there with a long face, not saying a word and saying you don't know what's wrong and you don't know what to do. I don't know what to do!" Then Willa sat down on the rug in the middle of the living room floor and cried.

Emily was shocked. Willa rarely cried. She put her arms around Willa and whispered against the side of her head. "I'm sorry. Willa, I'm so sorry. I don't want you to suffer too." And Emily cried for the first time, letting some of her desperation escape through barely-controlled sobs.

Afterwards, they talked. Willa made a pot of lemon tea and they cuddled one another on the love seat.

"What can I do to help?" Willa said in a voice alive with hope. She smiled and stroked Emily's hands and her face.

Emily bent her head away from Willa's smile and hands and felt tears coming again. "I don't know. I don't know what I can do." She squeezed Willa's hand and held it tightly. "I wish I did. There's got to be more to my life than this, that's all I know."

Nothing felt right in her life, she told Willa as she sipped lemon tea. Even her relationship with Willa had become mundane. "We never talk, really talk to each other," she said, starting to cry again. "We coexist. We're not intimate. We don't have any passion between us. Do you know what I mean?"

Willa held her tightly.

She loved Willa. There was no question of that. But they were occupied with trivial concerns about when and where to do the grocery shopping, and the amount of the hydro bill and the phone bill, and mechanical problems with the car. She remembered the excitement of their first months together and she wanted that thrilling intimacy again. Was that too much to expect? She said all this to Willa. Her desperation made her truthful. And she was relieved to see Willa nodding as if she understood, as if she agreed.

"Work," Emily said, blowing her nose and wiping her eyes. "Work is deadly. I hate it!"

She went over her work history, describing it for Willa as if Willa did not know, starting as a receptionist then moving to acting pay clerk and then permanent pay clerk and now a staffing officer. Each job was interesting for a while. In the beginning there were things to learn: forms, regulations, new problems to solve, new people to work with. But the work always became tedious once she mastered it.

"Mistressed it," Willa said.

They giggled together. Emily poured another round of lemon tea.

She did wonder, from time to time, if she wanted upward mobility. It would mean more money. But the last step upward, to staffing officer, had changed her working life drastically. Her supervisor was a man, although more enlightened and open than many men. The majority of people throughout the department who were involved in making decisions about staffing were men. Did she want this for the rest of her life? Some women were able to do it, were able to get along with the men. Why couldn't she?

Emily started to cry again. "I feel like a heartless woman. And it's true, you know. I've reached the end. It doesn't matter if I know the work or can do the job. Without a university degree I can't go any farther than this. My work is so boring. My whole life is boring!"

"Let's make a list," Willa said, "of your options. What can you do? What would you like to do? You need to consider some changes and do some planning." She got a piece of paper and a pen. "Say any old thing. Okay? Nothing's too outrageous."

Emily sniffed and wiped the tears from her cheeks. Willa and her lists. She watched Willa write the words.

"It's not a very long list."

"You could have a baby."

"Isn't that what straight couples do to save their relationships? A baby would really change our lives." Emily giggled. "Why not. Add it to the list."

"What about painting? That one of yours over our bed is very good. You have talent."

Emily was silent for a minute. Then she said, "Sure, why not."

"We'll put the list on the fridge, okay? And you can add things as you think of them."

Emily read the list twice before going to bed.

1. go to university
2. buy a house
3. find another job
4. take a holiday
5. quit work and live on unemployment
6. have a baby
7. paint

In bed that night, her arm resting along Willa's hip, she realized the depression was still with her. The evening of tears and earnest conversation with Willa had not helped. The list hadn't made a difference. Emily felt betrayed and more desperate than ever.

But the next morning, staring at the list on the fridge door as she made a cheese and lettuce sandwich for lunch, she decided the list might be a good idea. She phoned Carleton University during her morning coffee break and asked to have application forms for admission mailed to her.

She felt a little less desperate for a few days as she waited for the forms to arrive. Once the forms were filled out and mailed, and money sent to her high school so a transcript of marks would be mailed to Carleton, she waited. Waiting seemed worse than anything she had endured so far. Her whole future, her very life, revolved around being accepted by Carleton University. Having

made her decision, she wanted their decision to arrive by
return mail.

She wondered what she would do if she was accepted,
she confided to Willa. Since the crying session on the
living room floor, they were talking more frequently to
one another about their feelings and thoughts. Emily
wondered if it would last, the intimacy she remembered
from their early days together, but hurried past that
thought each time it tried to surface.

Willa led her to the kitchen and pointed, wordlessly, at
the list on the fridge. Emily felt like crumpling the piece
of paper into a tiny tight ball.

The next day she started actively looking for a new job.
A lateral transfer to another department was unlikely,
especially since the recent cutbacks and the freeze on
hiring. Still, she looked at the bulletin board in the hall
outside her office every morning. It was enough to depress
her, if she wasn't already depressed.

She started buying a newspaper on her way home
from work and reading the want ads every evening. Every
so often there was a job opportunity, but private sector
organizations wanted people with degrees for personnel
positions. And most companies offered salaries and benefits that were significantly less than what she had.

She stayed in the office after work every day for a week
and used the computer to work on her resumé. Then she
mailed the resumé with a covering letter to every possible
job prospect — even when a degree was a requirement,
even when bilingualism was essential. It was a discourag-
ing process. Most companies did not have the courtesy to
acknowledge receiving her application or send her a rejection letter. Those few that did reply sent cold and imper-

sonal form letters.

One day would haunt Emily forever. The day she threw the mug across the kitchen.

Emily arrived home from work that day and found a solitary brown envelope in the mail box. She reached for it eagerly and turned it over. The telephone bill. She climbed the stairs to the apartment, went into the kitchen and stood staring at the brown envelope in her right hand. Feelings of desperation welled up in her and she threw the envelope at the table. It landed on the floor, beneath the table. She left it there and made herself a cup of coffee.

Emily sat at the kitchen table, sipping coffee and looking around the room. Neat and tidy. Willa kept everything in its place. The herbs and spices were lined up in little brown bottles along four narrow wooden shelves. Basil, cinnamon, chili powder, curry, dill seeds, ginger, marjoram, mustard, oregano, thyme . . . she looked at the envelope lying on the beige and white linoleum floor.

If Carleton didn't accept her, what then? She couldn't do anything until she heard from them. Her life was on hold while she waited. Why was it taking so long? And what would she do if they rejected her?

She drank the last of the coffee and looked again at the rows of bottles. What was the difference, anyway, between a herb and a spice? She imagined herself picking up each bottle and dropping it on the floor, one by one, bottles crashing and breaking on the spotless beige and white floor, making a small mountain of herbs and spices and broken glass. The colours would mingle, yellows and oranges and browns and greens, and the smells would be strong. She felt like laughing, like throwing her head back and howling at the ceiling.

She heard a door open and close. Willa peeked around the door frame. "Hi. Have a good day?"

"I haven't heard from Carleton. Not a word!" She reached for the empty mug and threw it at the list on the refrigerator door. The mug hit the door, missing the list by inches, and shattered, flinging pieces of china in all directions. One large piece landed on the brown envelope under the table.

Emily stared at the piece of china on the envelope and Willa stared at Emily.

"O-kay," Willa said.

Emily looked at Willa. "It's the waiting, the not knowing. It's driving me crazy. What will I do if they don't accept me?" Her voice was loud, almost screaming.

"You'll get in. They will accept you. Don't make yourself sick about it. It's not worth it."

"What if they don't?"

"If they don't, they don't. You'll do something else."

Willa got the broom and swept the pieces of china into a tidy pile. Emily watched Willa's strong hands and felt remorse. Willa was cleaning up her mess. It wasn't fair. Nothing in the whole world was fair.

"Willa?" What could she say? To apologize seemed inadequate.

Willa closed the garbage can and turned to Emily. "Yes?"

What could she say? The question echoed through her mind, searching for an answer. "Wil, I'm sorry." There, she'd said it and it was inadequate.

Willa sat at the table, across from Emily.

"What's going on? I know you're sorry. The mug doesn't matter. But the violence of your feelings . . . I want

147

to help you, but I can't do anything about what you are doing to yourself. I get scared too. Everyone gets scared. You can't give in to it. And you can't give up. It'll change again. You'll feel better."

Emily looked at Willa's face and down to the strong hands clasping one another. She looked at her own hands, laying passively in her lap, and back to Willa's face.

Emily closed her eyes. She couldn't say anything to Willa, couldn't open her mouth and let the words escape. She was sorry for throwing the mug but at the same time she wanted to drag a piece of the broken glass along the soft part of Willa's arm and to carve bloody lines on Willa's face. She couldn't say that when she closed her eyes she saw broken glass and spices all over the floor and wondered what it meant. It was not like her to be violent. What did the vision mean? Was it going to happen one day just as she saw it when she closed her eyes? Was she going to lose control?

"Phone Carleton. Do it now!"

Emily opened her eyes and looked at her wrist watch. "They'll be closed."

"Phone!"

Emily went into the living room. She found the phone number in the white pages of the telephone book and dialled and listened to the ringing. Seven times it rang before a voice answered.

"Hello. I want to find out if my application has been accepted . . . Yes, I know, but . . . Emily Buchanan . . . Thank you . . . Yes, yes, that's right, yes . . . I have? Really? Thanks. Thanks! When will I . . . Thank you . . . of course. Goodbye."

Willa laughed when Emily told her. "There, you see. I

told you so. I said there was nothing to worry about."

"Yes, you did."

Everything would be alright now. Why didn't she feel the satisfaction she had expected? Is this what she wanted? Years in university? Debt? Why did she want to cry?

And she kept thinking about the mug. In the following days that memory haunted her, intensifying her sense of desperation and the terror which ruled her. She was a pacifist so where did they come from, those feelings? Had these explosive feelings been in her all the time, her whole life, waiting for a chance to get out?

Emily cried often, in secret and for no apparent reason. Sometimes she would cry every day. Sometimes twice or three times in a day. She always managed to control the urge to cry until she could be alone, because she was ashamed of her tears.

And when she fell asleep, and some nights it took hours, it was as if she waged exhausting battles all night long. She never woke in the morning feeling rested and refreshed. Most mornings she had to force herself to get out of bed. She felt tired all day, day after day, always tired. Getting through each day required effort, more effort than she felt capable of gathering together. There were moments, especially in the middle of the night, when she wondered why she bothered trying.

Her internal world was in chaos, causing her to doubt every feeling, to question her values, to wonder at her thoughts, to despise herself. She felt she did not know herself any more and could not trust herself. She avoided mirrors because the woman facing her was frightening. Eyes stared back, expressionless. Skin was sickly. Hair was straggly. Her expression was bleak. She expected others to look at her and see a shallow, insecure woman, to see that she was incompetent and inadequate and unattractive and know she was falling apart.

Emily knew she had to do something. She thought and thought and finally she decided to talk to Sheila.

She phoned Sheila and they arranged to meet for lunch at a downtown cafe. Sheila would be safe. She never saw herself doing violent things to Sheila.

When they met, she was feeling weak and vulnerable and something (pride? fear?) prevented her from revealing all her thoughts and feelings. "I've resigned from my job," she said. Her stomach jumped and turned as she said the words aloud. Anxiety, she thought, was becoming a way of life.

Emily talked about how frightening it was to give up the financial security of her job, the agony of trying to decide which university courses to take, the high cost of tuition and books. Emily didn't mention throwing the mug or wanting to carve bloody lines on Willa's face. She said nothing about the visions of broken glass and spices all over the kitchen floor.

"Some nights," Emily said, her voice getting louder, "I can't get to sleep until two or three and even then I toss and turn and wake up feeling tired. I'm always tired." Emily realized she was speaking loudly and lowered her voice. "Willa says I'm keeping her up when I'm so restless. But I tell her it's her imagination." She can't bear to admit her behaviour is affecting Willa, can't bear to feel responsible for anything else going wrong. But this too she did not say to Sheila.

"Aren't you going to eat your salad?"

Emily looked down at the plate. "No. I'm not very

hungry."

Sheila reached for the plate. "You're still depressed. Those are the symptoms. Insomnia, loss of appetite. It starts with anger and you turn the anger in on yourself instead of expressing it and so you get depressed."

"If the depression is caused by anger, where did the anger come from?" Emily's voice was steady and cold. "What am I angry about? Tell me how I can be angry and not know I'm angry?"

"Do you want more coffee?" Sheila caught the waiter's eye and pointed at her empty coffee cup. "I don't know. You have to answer those questions. You must know somewhere within yourself."

Maybe she was right. But Emily wanted something more from her friend. She wanted Sheila to hear her despair. She wanted understanding, empathy, a hug that would make her feel safe. Emily wanted to yell at Sheila, wanted to sneer at her. All her fine words, sounding profound. She wanted to lean across the table and slap Sheila, a hard slap that would make Sheila's head jerk and stop her useless words. One slap so hard that her own hand would ache afterwards.

She immediately hated herself for wanting to hurt Sheila. A moment later she hated Sheila for . . . for what? She looked at her watch and told Sheila she had to leave or she would be late for work.

Emily began to avoid Sheila. Willa didn't seem to notice or if she did she didn't say anything. Sheila didn't call, but then that wasn't uncommon as it was usually Emily who phoned and made arrangements for them to meet.

Emily told herself no one could give her everything she

needed, not all the time, and she was expecting too much of her friend. Then she hated herself a little more for wanting Sheila to be perfect and for feeling her friend had failed her. But still, she resented Sheila's smooth and empty words. She felt Sheila had betrayed their friendship. She had asked Sheila for help and it had been a very difficult thing to do and surely she deserved more from her friend.

Gradually Emily discovered that she missed Sheila, missed their cosy conversations and their unspoken affection and their laughing fits over the behaviour of mutual friends. She missed the security of being with a friend who knew her well and cared for her.

When she finally phoned Sheila, her friend's voice sounded warm. This conversation was different. Sheila listened and asked questions. She gave Emily all her attention.

Sheila said, "Aw, you poor kid."

Then she said, "It sounds like some kind of living hell."

Sheila said she was worried about her. That was what Emily wanted to hear. Someone was worried about her. Emily was very worried about herself.

Sheila said, "You know I love you. What can I do for you? Tell me, won't you."

Emily made mistakes as she tried to regain control over her life. Quitting the government job seemed like a mistake. It wasn't a mistake, not really. It was an attempt to do something for herself, to change her life and feel in control. But it wasn't the answer. And quitting her job gave her something new to worry about. Money.

Attending university kept her busy, although it

brought new frustrations and anxieties. Initially she felt challenged. She met new people, although most of the other students were years younger. But as the weeks passed, Emily started to question the purpose of school and wondered about the kind of learning demanded from her. She had expected that working toward getting a degree would give her a sense of fulfilment. Instead, she listened as white middle-class men slanted the subjects they taught with their biases and personal views while presenting the information as fact. To add to Emily's frustration, they revealed their sexist attitudes almost every time they moved their lips.

Her anger came alive in Introduction to Psychology. Homosexuality was presented with theories about why people become homosexual. Emily's feelings jumped between rage and hatred. Mostly she felt helpless. She chose to write her mid-term essay on theories about why people become heterosexual and, although she knew it was carefully researched (Sheila helped her with the research) and well-written (Willa helped her with the writing), the instructor returned it with a failing mark.

That scared her, the possibility of failing a course. The reason she was at university, and in debt, was to get a degree.

Nevertheless, she was too occupied with school work — attending classes, researching and writing essays, reading text books, studying for exams — to think about her ever-present depression. That was one advantage of being at university. She had little time to think of anything except school.

Emily continued to read the want ads in the newspaper and occasionally applied for a job. She wondered, each time she composed a letter to accompany her resumé, why she was applying for a job when she was going to university. It seemed to be a compulsion, a need to explore every possibility.

Willa occasionally nagged her to remember the last item on the list. But Emily was too busy to think about painting.

"And anyway," she said to Willa, "I haven't painted for years. I wouldn't know where to begin or how to do it."

She studied for final exams, resenting this method of measuring what she had learned, knowing she would not be tested on her ability to understand and apply concepts but on her ability to memorize and regurgitate certain details to suit the individual needs of each tester. It was a game and she resented it, but she tried her best to win.

After the stress of final exams, a new fear ruled her. She had to decide whether to return to university or find something else to do. She had quit her job and now she wanted to quit university. Was she one of those people that never stick at anything? And what would she do about money? She would have to get a job. Another boring government job? She did not want that. But what did she want?

She had not been raised to make these kinds of decisions. This was what she said to Willa one day. "I was brought up to be a wife and mother, in that order. I wasn't socialized to take work seriously or to think about any career except being a homemaker. I wasn't brought up to worry my pretty little head about what I'll do for the rest of my life." She laughed, a short laugh. "Now I know I will always work. I'll always have to support myself. Still, I'm just learning to be serious about it. At the age of thirty.

Can you believe it?"

Willa sighed. "It's true. My mother wanted me to take a secretarial course after high school. Thank the goddess my aunt talked me into going to university."

Emily rubbed her hand across her face. "I feel so aimless. What will I be when I grow up?"

"You can be anything you want. Except it's a little late to become a ballerina."

"Yes." Emily gave another short laugh. But what did she want to be? Surely that was a question for a fifteen-year-old or an eighteen-year-old, not for an adult woman.

Willa was right. She could be anything she wanted, do whatever she wished.

The next morning, after Willa had left for work, Emily sat at the kitchen table. Still in her pyjamas because she did not have a reason to get dressed, she nursed a mug of lukewarm coffee and stared at the trees across the road. The building was silent and the street was deserted. Everyone had something to do, somewhere to be. Everyone but her. She was all alone, with no direction. Tears filled her eyes and slid down the curves of her cheeks. This can't go on.

She whispered the words out loud.

"This can't go on."

The aching and trembling in her belly and chest released a sob: the sob broke the silence of the apartment and the sound echoed in her head. Another sob broke loose, louder than the first. She buried her face in her hands and cried, ragged sounds increasing in number and force. She cried louder, enjoying the noise of her pain. Mucous from her nose mingled with the warm tears.

Afterwards, she sat on the toilet seat and washed her

face with warm water. Then she took a shower. She stretched and turned as the pellets of hot water soothed her body. She lingered, reluctant to leave although she regretted the waste of water.

Two weeks later she started her summer job, working as a staffing officer in her old office while her former colleagues took their holidays. It was familiar and safe — the faces, the routines, the expectations. Emily was amazed at how easily she remembered the forms and procedures. Nothing had changed.

She had used up all her savings during the months at university and the security of an income every two weeks boosted her spirits. But being there reminded her that she didn't want to be there. She consoled herself with the thought that it was a summer job. She did not have to stay forever. And, she reminded herself, the pay was good.

On Tuesday, her second day back at her old job, Emily realized she was resisting urges to cry, urges to cry for no good reason. She was determined to feel better so on Thursday she bought a bottle of wine at lunchtime.

Willa arrived home at her usual time and took a glass of white wine with one hand and, much to Emily's surprise, gave her a gift with the other. Emily held the silver and blue package for a moment, grinning at Willa, knowing it was a book. Then she ripped open the paper. *Emily Carr* by Doris Shadbolt.

She leafed through the pages. "*Emily Carr* and with colour plates. Thank you, Willa." She picked up her wine glass and held it out toward Willa. "Thanks, you."

They smiled at one another, two mouths stretching with pleasure.

"I'll wash the breakfast dishes while you look at it."

Little Scraps and Nothingnesses

Emily opened the book. There was a quotation in Willa's handwriting on the inside cover.

It was these tiny things that, collectively, taught me how to live. Too insignificant to have been considered individually . . . the little scraps and nothingnesses of my life have made a definite pattern.

— Emily Carr

"Sometimes," Emily had been known to say to Willa, "it's as if you read my mind and know exactly what I'm thinking or needing." She thought of that as she looked at Willa's long back bent over the sink and a rush of warm feelings ran through her. Willa was a special woman, loyal and calm and loving.

"You are a special woman."

Willa turned. "Do you like Emily Carr?"

"How could I not like my namesake?" Emily brushed her fingertips back and forth over the cover of the book. "Those of us with the same name have a connection. But I don't know much about her. When we studied Canadian Art in high school we studied the Group of Seven as if those boys were the only important artists in the country."

"I looked through the book when I bought it. There's one there, a painting of dark colours titled *Grey* and it has a female feeling. It's a tree but like the shape of a wedge of pie, if you can picture that, and kinda reminds me of a vagina. Want me to find it for you?"

Emily nodded.

It was a wonderful evening of laughter and harmony, but the next morning Emily woke with the old ghosts haunting her.

She could hear Willa washing in the bathroom, getting ready to go to work. "Willa!" She sat up in bed. "Willa, what if I don't go back to university?"

Willa stood in the doorway of the bedroom, naked, brushing her hair. "Jeez, Emily. Your life will go on. Don't go back if you don't want to but you'd better get moving right now or you're going to be late for work."

At lunchtime Emily closed the door to her office and ate an egg sandwich while reading the book about Emily Carr. Born December 13, 1871. A Sagittarius. In 1910, at the age of 39, she travelled to France to study art. And then did very little painting from 1913 to 1927. She returned to painting when she was 56.

Emily had to close the book when she read that part because she was sure she would cry if she kept reading. She sat, staring at the sky beyond her window. All those lost years when Emily Carr's creative energy had been diverted into supporting herself and surviving as best she could. No patrons for her. The wealthy and influential men were patronizing the male artists back East. How did she keep going when there was complete lack of recognition for her work? How was her creative spirit able to flourish in poverty? It required a single-mindedness, a strong belief in self.

Emily opened the book and continued reading.

In 1921 the National Gallery of Canada declined an opportunity to buy some of Emily Carr's paintings. In 1944, at age 73, after two heart attacks and two strokes, she still painted and wrote books. The determination of the woman. Emily doubted she could do it. It would take more determination and strength than she possessed.

Sheila knocked on the door and walked in as Emily was studying the painting on the cover of the book — a blue sky that reminded Emily of the ocean.

"Hi! What are you doing here?"

"Come to see you, dear kid."

She sat down across from Emily's desk and told Emily the recent gossip from their circle of friends and then raved about her visit to an astrologer. She urged Emily to see the woman.

"Astrology's a science," Sheila assured Emily. "Maybe she could tell you what to do. You never know. It might help."

Sheila gave her the astrologer's phone number and address before leaving.

Emily thought about the astrologer all afternoon while she worked. Why not? It suited her mood these days. It couldn't do any harm and, as Sheila said, it might help.

The summer passed slowly. Emily met Sheila, by chance, as she was walking from work to the bus stop one day in early August.

"Emily! I've been thinking about you lately and meaning to call to have lunch or something. Have you decided what to do?"

Emily shook her head. "My job ends next week and they've offered me a term position. I don't think I want to go back to Carleton, but I don't know what to do."

"Did you ever go to see that astrologer?"

"No. To be quite honest, I'd forgotten all about her."

"Go see her, why don't you. Just for fun. It may be the best thing you do for yourself this year. You know, kid, you never can tell. Do you still have her number?"

Emily phoned the astrologer when she got home and

made an appointment for the end of August.

Willa was sceptical. "Why don't you do something constructive, like volunteering with the sexual assault centre or something. You're wasting your money on that stuff, just throwing it away."

Emily shrugged. "Why not? I might as well enjoy the money I earn. I've decided to take the term position. I'm going to have money to spare."

"Don't help her. It's a racket. Don't tell her anything about yourself. Don't give anything away. Don't go there wearing rings or jewellery and don't carry anything."

"Willa, seriously. It's not like you to be suspicious."

"I don't want you to be hurt. I don't want you to get your hopes up for nothing. They say the same thing to everyone and it's so general it could apply to anyone."

Emily was nervous the morning of her appointment with the astrologer. It took forty minutes to decide what to wear, and then she changed her mind and went through the whole process again. She was finally dressed and ready to leave two hours before the appointed time. She took a book from the book case, the one on Emily Carr, and leafed through the pages. She forgot about the time and then had to race around and leave for the appointment in a great rush.

She was ten minutes late when she arrived at the high-rise apartment building. The astrologer responded promptly to Emily's knock and gave her a broad smile.

"Hello. You're Emily? I'm Caitlin. Come in."

She led Emily to the living room, which was cluttered with paper and books. Caitlin looked to be in her late forties, maybe early fifties. She was barefoot, dressed in blue corduroy trousers and an over-sized green shirt.

Emily was disappointed. She had expected something exotic, a dark room crammed with bizarre furniture and a woman with an accent and a turban on her head, wearing multi-coloured bracelets and necklaces.

Lifting a sheet of paper, which was encased in plastic, Caitlin handed it to Emily. "This is your chart. It shows the positions of the planets at the time of your birth."

Emily accepted the sheet and looked at it. Two circles, one within the other, intersecting lines dividing the circles into pie wedges, strange symbols, numbers . . . none of it had any meaning for her.

"Sit down here, beside me, why don't you."

Emily sat on the chair Caitlin had indicated and carefully placed the plasticised sheet on her lap.

"Have you been to an astrologer before?"

"No."

Caitlin looked pleased. "I thought you hadn't. You didn't know the time of your birth." She opened a small book of what appeared to be mathematical tables and rested one hand on the open pages. She started to talk, occasionally looking down at the book, telling Emily details from her childhood and early twenties. Emily was silent, rarely moving in the chair. The insights of this stranger amazed her.

Then Caitlin said, "This is a special time for you. The first Saturn return. Are you finding it difficult?"

"Yes." Emily was reluctant to reveal much about herself, in case it was all trickery as Willa said.

"Yes. Saturn is moving to the same place it was when you were born. It's a slow-moving planet. This is the first time it's returned to the same position it was in at your birth. It's a major landmark in your life, a time of changes, great changes, immense and frightening changes. Change is the key word. Change and growth. It's a time to examine yourself, the values you have accumulated from childhood, and to begin to truly know yourself and to test and stretch your limits. You need to refocus the direction of your life. It may manifest itself in a career change or having a baby or deciding not to have children. You may settle into a long-term relationship. Or end one. It's a marvellous time. If you don't deny your emotions." She paused and looked at Emily.

Emily, for the first time, looked at Caitlin's grey-black eyes and smiled a genuine smile. "That's what's happening to me. I've been depressed and I quit my job and went to university and now I've quit university and gone back to my job. I don't know what to do any more."

"Yes. This is an insecure time and very confusing. A time of growth, for examining the past and moving beyond it, a time of transformation. There's deep pain with the growth."

Emily nodded. "I know. Nothing makes sense. I feel lost."

"Yes, you have a tendency to be intellectual. Don't deny your emotions. You need your emotional side too. Feel. Explore your feelings and learn to trust them."

"I don't know what I'm feeling, except confused."

Caitlin smiled, a broad smile. The lines around her eyes and mouth deepened and stretched. "You're getting ready. It'll become clear to you. Don't be intimidated by your confusion. It's part of your maturation, learning to know yourself. You are restructuring your life, throwing out the old and taking in the new. It's not easy. You must trust yourself, trust your sixth sense. We all have it, but it's strong in you. Go deeper into whatever is important to you."

"How much longer will this take?"

"We spend our whole lives growing and learning. But this acute period will last twelve more months for you, until this time next year."

"Twelve more months!"

"Yes, but it won't all be like this. Already you feel better, don't you? It's getting better. You will feel more sureness and confidence and you will learn your strengths. Do you have a companion?"

"Yes."

"Do you talk? Is he supporting you through this?"

"She. She's a she."

Caitlin didn't speak for a moment, then laughed. "You young people are refreshing with your openness and honesty. Is she giving you support?"

Emily grinned, nodding her head slowly. "When she can."

Afterwards Emily felt a need to think and reflect on everything Caitlin had said. She walked home, although it was almost three miles, and smiled absent-mindedly at the strangers she passed on the sidewalk. She was amazed that Caitlin, a stranger, had understood what she was going through. Could the position of a particular planet influence her life? Maybe there was something to this astrology stuff. And somehow, she couldn't say exactly how, Caitlin had made her feel special.

Emily almost skipped for joy as she walked. Perhaps a fresh start would make her feel better. She had been fantasizing about moving for months, trying to picture herself living in Toronto or Winnipeg or Vancouver. But she lacked the energy and the inner motivation to look for a place to live, move her possessions, find a job, learn her way around a new city, and find new friends. And anyway it would be difficult, perhaps impossible, to persuade Willa to move. She was not prepared to leave Willa.

She was exhausted when she got home.

An envelope was waiting in the mail box. Emily dialled Sheila's number while opening the envelope.

"Hello. It's me . . . I saw your astrologer today, Caitlin . . . Yes. She's a gorgeous woman . . . a lot of things. I need time to think about them . . . yes, yes, Sheila, you were right. It was worth it. And I just got a rejection letter for a job I applied to, administrator of some arts group . . . well, I'll apply for almost anything. I have another job interview, for a new health centre for women, on Wednesday . . . Okay, let's have lunch. Are you free Thursday? . . . okay . . . okay, yes, see you there at noon. Bye."

She ripped the rejection letter into small pieces and threw the bits into the garbage.

Emily looks up at the overcast sky. Dear Wil. She imagines Willa sitting in the old green boat, joking with her sister Ruth about the best kind of bait, whispering so their father won't notice and yell at them for scaring off the fish.

Cuddling this morning before they got out of bed, before that strange feeling came over Emily as she searched for the yellow sweat shirt, Willa spoke aloud the thoughts that were going through Emily's mind.

"I cherish you." Willa planted little kisses across Emily's forehead. "It's mixed up in my head, what's been going on. But I feel you're over that."

Emily hugged Willa, squeezing her tightly so that Willa said, "Hey, I can't breath."

Willa. She loved that name. She called her Wicked Willy when she was in a playful mood.

She had thought about leaving Willa during those hellish months. Emily went from one extreme to the other: feeling her life would end if she left Willa; feeling she must leave Willa to save herself and to regain control of her life. Unable to love herself, Emily could not love Willa. But to leave would have been a catastrophe, not a mere mistake. Somehow she had been able to recognize that much, no matter how desperate she felt.

Leaving Willa was not a new thought. It had occurred to her every once in a while through the years when things were messy between them. Willa, she knew, also thought about leaving. She was amazed that Willa had stayed with her through the depression, amazed that Willa didn't get completely fed up and lose hope. If their places were reversed, would she have stayed? She didn't know and this was another reason to hate herself.

Were the mistakes necessary, a part of the process of finding her way out of despair? Mistake was not the right word. Quitting her job had been necessary to bring about the other changes. It was not a mistake, not a failure, not something to regret. It was not the solution, either. Each decision was an attempt to feel better about herself, a stumbling step to find the right direction.

Finally, when she was ready to give up all hope, she began to feel better.

The transition from despair to confidence seemed to happen quickly, over a few weeks. Or was it a few days?

After the frightening months that stretched on forever, her frustration slowly evaporated into the humid summer air.

Then she started thinking about painting again and began to feel better almost as soon as she realized she wanted to paint. Willa had urged her to paint throughout the long months of despair but Emily resisted the idea. It was a ridiculous notion. She was sure it would be a waste, a complete waste of time and money and energy. She would feel like a failure and for what? And thus she ignored Willa's advice and kept her mind closed to the idea.

Until one day when she was running through Beechwood Cemetery. After three days of rain she was impatient to be running again. Her body was heavy, her breathing was laboured and every step required concentrated effort. At the top of the hill which led into the cemetery she slowed down to a walk for a few yards, then continued running.

She ran the length of the cemetery and circled back, forcing herself to keep going. It was a struggle, increasingly difficult, until she had to stop running and bend forward, massaging a stitch in her side. As she massaged, she took slow deep breaths . . . in, one, two, three, four, five, six . . . out, one, two, three, four, five, six . . . in, one, two . . . she stood up gradually. Upright, she threw back her head to take a full breath of air. Exhaling with exaggerated slowness, she opened her eyes and saw the huge maple tree.

It was majestic. The ground around the tree was covered with drying, dark crimson leaves. Near the ground the thick trunk divided into several stout, ascending branches to form a symmetrical oval-shaped crown. The leaves of the lower branches represented the colours of autumn, an array of bright red through fiery orange to lemony yellow. The upper branches were bare.

She looked around at the other maple trees. Nearly all of them had leaves of one colour. Bright red was the most common. This huge tree was the only one with leaves of brilliant oranges and yellows.

Emily sat on the grass, at the edge of the narrow dirt road, and a strong urge came over her — a desire to paint this scene. It would make a splendid painting, the vibrant trees dominating the picture with carefully cultivated grass and aging headstones in the foreground.

She started sketching, in her mind. She pencilled an outline of the maple, placing it in the foreground, a little to the left of centre. She drew other, less-distinguished trees behind the magnificent maple, and then a border of headstones along the immediate foreground.

It doesn't matter where you put the centre of interest, she thought as she studied the tree, as long as it is the centre of interest. That was something her high school art teacher used to say.

Moving in her mind from the working sketch she began with a wash of transparent french ultramarine for the sky, leaving white spaces for dabs of vermilion and cadmium yellow. She used a red-sable brush with a needle-sharp point to draw the maple. The limbs arched outward and upwards, firm strokes, spreading into the shape of a full-bodied crown.

Emily looked down at her idle hands and then over at the tree. Shaking her head slightly from side to side, she stood up. She couldn't do it. It had been too long. She hadn't painted since high school. Thirteen years. She'd turn everything to mud. It was one thing to do it in her head. That was easy. But she couldn't make it happen on paper.

She walked over to a low headstone, swung her leg upward and brought it gently down, resting her heel on the flat top. Leaning forward, in a scissor-like motion, she wrapped her fingers around her ankle. She held the position, counting to thirty, delighting in the feeling of her muscles expanding and stretching almost to the point of pain. She went through the same process with her other leg.

Maybe Willa was right, maybe she should try painting again. Relearning the skills would be frustrating but she would get better if she kept at it. Emily Carr had done it, had lived an adventurous life and been true to her heart's desire. She went to France to study art when she was 39 years old. Emily was a mere 30.

She stood at attention, then shook her whole body before walking across the grass, carefully skirting the plots where the earth was sinking, to the majestic tree. Her fingertips touched the trunk, lightly, then she placed both palms against the uneven bark. A wave of excitement surged through her. A feeling came with it, a sense that she knew what she wanted and it waited for her just beyond the next moment.

She stepped back and pushed the tree, then pressed the length of her body against the sturdy trunk. The rough hard bark felt solid.

She resumed running without a backward glance, maintaining a vigorous pace. Her body was moving with ease and her breathing was regular. She would paint herself hugging a tree. It could be the basis for a series of paintings, she thought, a variation on Marion Engel's novel

Bear. Woman develops sensuous relationship with a sugar maple. She had hugged a tree! She shook her head as she ran, laughing silently at herself.

She would bring Willa here, after supper, and show her the tree. She decided to walk the rest of the way home. It seemed the right thing to do, to slow down and take her time.

Just a week later, when she was offered the job as coordinator of the women's health clinic, she knew this was another turning point in her life. She was excited and happy and hopeful and confident. She felt like a real woman entitled to a proper place in the world. When she told Willa about the job offer, she threw her arms around her and squeezed until darling Wil said, "Hey, you're hurting me with love."

Emily stepped back, holding Willa's hands, laughing. "Let's go out for dinner. My treat! We have to celebrate!"

Willa hugged Emily and whispered in her ear, "My pretty one, you are precious."

Emily puts her mug on the window ledge and sits on the wooden chair. She will start the new job next week. That thought warms her. She is looking forward to being part of the beginnings of this unique clinic, the first of its kind in the city. And she feels good about her ability to do the job. The clinic will open in three weeks. Nine women — two nurses, a social worker, a physiotherapist, a dentist, a receptionist, a doctor, a bookkeeper, and a masseuse. Ten, counting herself. All women. She is especially thrilled at the prospect of working in an all-women environment.

There will be problems, there are always problems.

But working through them will be part of the challenge of the job. She will deal with each issue as it occurs. She is eager to start the job and excited about meeting the other staff. This job will have lots of variety and will never be boring. Life is wonderful!

Money. That is her only concern. The coordinator's salary is less than she was earning in her government job. Nothing is perfect. The low salary means she will not own a country retreat like Sheila's cottage. Her daydream will remain a fantasy. But life is filled with trade-offs. Job satisfaction is far more important than salary or benefits.

Is she fooling herself? Is working at a women's health clinic really more worthwhile than working for the government or for some corporation? She wrinkles her nose, as if at an unpleasant smell. Of course it will be more fulfilling to work at the clinic. Far far better to work at a job that helps other women directly. Far better to work in an organization that recognizes and supports the needs of women and works to change the social structure. It's alright for those women who want to work for the government or corporations. Like Sheila, directing an equal opportunity program in her government department. And Willa, working at a local radio station, lobbying to get them to hire a woman disc jockey, to play more music by women, and learning how to survive in a male-dominated industry. They like what they are doing, in spite of the frustrations, and they are working to change their work environments.

They make more money and have good benefits and pension plans. Other than that, there is no comparison. Wages and benefits. She bends forward, resting her chin in her right hand. Money.

Why does a government-funded organization have to pay dreadful wages? One of her goals at the clinic will be to increase staff salaries. She had decided that already, after reviewing the annual budget with the President when they met to sign her employment contract. The President agreed, Yes, increasing the salaries for staff must be a priority. Emily decided at that moment that she liked the President and it confirmed her sense that she is going to like this job.

She has another concern. Being a lesbian among non-lesbians. This is not really a problem. It is more an ongoing part of her life — coming out to other women. It becomes an issue from time to time but Emily will have to go through the process and see what develops. Perhaps there is a dyke, or even two, among the staff. The President of the Board is a dyke. Emily met her for the first time at the job interview, but knew of her through mutual friends. The President and the rest of the hiring committee know Emily is a dyke, because on her resumé she included volunteer experience from a few years ago, fund-raising for a lesbian magazine. She is relieved to be out to her employers. One less worry in the new job.

This was something new in her life, a decision that evolved out of the months of depression, to include lesbian-related work experience on her resume. She had been apprehensive about taking the risk. Jobs were lost for less. But as she said to Willa, more to reassure herself than to hear Willa applaud her stand, it was time to open the closet door a little wider.

A low salary and coming out to her co-workers, these are manageable concerns and do not inhibit the excitement she feels about her life. She is on the right path, after months of confusion. Or was it years? It seemed to go on forever, month after month of feeling helpless, months and months of not knowing what to do.

But that is behind her.

Tiny drops land gently on the window. Emily reaches for the mug and takes a sip. The cold tea is a surprise to her mouth. She turns to look at the alarm clock and discovers two hours have passed. She stands up slowly, stretching her body, then moves swiftly toward the counter, feeling guilty about wasting two hours.

Leaning against the sink, staring out the window, she listens to the sound of gentle rain. There is a stillness in the world, broken only by the occasional call of a bird. Willa spotted a loon on the lake yesterday afternoon and called Emily to the window. From time to time Emily hears a lonely cry. Is it the loon?

The rain increases, sounding urgent. She wonders if Willa is getting wet. Or is Willa oblivious to physical discomfort as she concentrates on catching fish?

Are the elusive sensations neither *déjà vu* nor premonition but part of another turning point? Could there be more to know? All these questions. Where are the answers! She decides to mention it to Willa tonight after supper, after her family leaves, and see what Willa thinks.

She hopes it won't be a supper of pickerel.

She puts the kettle on the stove and notices Willa's book on the counter, the knife handle protruding from the pages. She has been wondering what there is about this book to make Willa read with such intensity. While waiting for the kettle to boil, she flips the book over, careful to leave the knife in place, and reads the back cover.

The writer is a witch and has documented her experiences in this book. She has a spirit guide. "Her name is Hettie," Emily reads aloud, enjoying the sound of her voice in the silent room. "She is an old woman who comes to me in my night dreams. She replays past experiences and shows me new meanings. In other dreams, she guides me to decisions."

The kettle starts to whistle. Emily makes a fresh cup of tea. Leaning against the counter, cradling the hot mug with one hand, she turns the book over and studies the intricate design of swirling yellows and pinks on the front cover. She traces the swirls with one finger, wondering if she has a spirit guide.

An image comes to her of a gracious woman, short-haired, wearing crystal blue sweat pants and a matching sweat shirt with grubby white running shoes on her feet.

Emily turns from the counter, puts her mug on the table, and begins to arrange her painting tools. She hums as she works. It feels good to have a whole day to paint, to want to paint, to be in the country, and to be starting an interesting job next week. Is there a place in her life for a spirit guide? It appeals to her, the thought of conjuring up a guide whenever she feels the need.

She looks at the landscape from the picture window. The rain has stopped. She stands back to study the shifting shadows on the water, humming as she considers the colours she will use to reproduce the stormy lake. She will paint this scene, the continually moving water and the angry sky and the bare trees on the other side of the lake and the rain-streaked window. She wants to give the viewer the sensation of standing inside a room and looking out through a window to the world.

Emily chuckles and presses her face against the glass. It is good to be alive, even if winter is on the way. Sheila said she will understand the depression, one day. The desperate feelings from those long months are still vivid in Emily's mind and she wants to understand now.

What would her spirit guide say about it?

She imagines the short-haired goddess standing beside her and hears a voice whisper in her ear.

Paint.

She laughs, a long and joyous laugh.